A SLIVER OF TIME

A Tale of Mosquito Inlet

To George + Sally,
thank you for our friendship, and for
the many years you cared for our
city and the people in it,

J.S. Lavallee

A Sliver of Time is the sequel to
A Slice of Moon by J.S. Lavallee, which was
awarded two silver medals in the categories of
Adult Florida Fiction and Florida Young Adult Fiction
by the Florida Authors and Publishers Association
President's National Competition 2016.

This is a work of fiction. The events and characters
described in this book are fictitious, although the
history of Mosquito Inlet is well documented.

ISBN: 9798699176618
Independently published through KDP
Printed in the United States of America.

To Mom

Because, somehow, she'll know.

MY EYES TOLD YOU

My eyes told you everything, the whole of my being,
Each rise and fall, mistakes and all,
From the beginning.

They pled for you to feel me, devour me, steal me,
While my lips became immobile,
Unable to speak.

My heart and mind filled with you,
Ached for you, dreamt of you,
And enraptured in the moment,
Time,
It seemed,
Stood still.

Then, by some divine design,
With your eyes locked hard on mine,
I heard your eyes say silently,
Tell me everything.

J. S. Lavallee

A SLIVER OF TIME

In 1768 the tall timber and earthen walls that surrounded the city of St. Augustine gave those who lived there a sense of security, and for some, a feeling of empowerment, but the wall couldn't prevent war or acquisition.

Whenever the town changed nationality, many of its departing inhabitants left little behind for the new residents. Between battles and belligerence the two hundred year old town remained poor, and thieves were known to roam the dark alleys at night, but the beautiful harbor, the mild winters and the generous government land grants nearby lured adventurous colonists to settle in the city and in the neighboring territory.

Enticed to become indentured servants, fourteen hundred Europeans, mostly from Menorca, Greece, and Italy, crossed the sea on eight ships to colonize the largest grant of land in East Florida; Dr. Andrew Turnbull's New Smyrna Plantation at Mosquito Inlet, seventy miles south of St. Augustine.

Along with a hundred African slaves brought down from the colonies, the twelve hundred immigrants who survived the voyage began to build an immense indigo and cotton farming enterprise out of dense forest, dangerous swampland, and fields of sandy soil.

During trying days for the settlers of St. Augustine, and amidst the cruelty and starvation suffered by the servants and slaves of Mosquito Inlet, love, hope and sometimes a smile helped them to bravely go on.

1.

The air felt thick and smothering hot, and the young woman who stood among the throng of passengers on the deck of the tall ship thought it hard to breathe.

Solid framed but spare of flesh and slightly disheveled, Darian looked over the small city of St. Augustine with an air of determination and a certain sense of self-worth, in spite of her travel worn clothes and unkempt condition.

Her long brunette hair was loosely swept back and tied beneath a pale linen scarf, exposing a heart shaped face with a pleasing combination of full lips, hazel green eyes, and olive skin that had tanned to a deeper shade after she lost her hat to the wind in the middle of the sea weeks earlier.

During the four months since she left her island home in Greece, she'd sailed with stalwart courage through the monstrous swells of raging storms, while she held on below deck in battened down blackness.

She'd weathered the unnerving hush of an eerie becalming which had lasted for days, and she'd worried over the passengers who were stricken by disease, while she wept for those who had lost their lives.

Aside from that, and the general discomfort of living in the squalor of an overcrowded ship, she did her best to keep her spirits high, as did the others.

Regardless of their varied heritages, they had much in common for they'd all left a life of war, strife and starvation amid the exciting promises of beginning a better world and owning their own land after their terms of service.

While the majority spoke a Menorcan dialect of Spanish, some shared an assortment of the Mediterranean languages that were present among them, and there were those who endeavored to learn English or improve what they knew of it as they made the crossing, but the languages of music and dance were understood by all and frequently practiced.

Although St. Augustine was not their final destination, the ship had been held at anchor for almost a week. Most of the indentured servants were anxious to disembark, but they were kept on board by overseers, and their morning clamor had subsided to a low grumble as the increasing heat and humidity of the day wore on them.

Darian heard someone proclaim that an assembly of settlers would be permitted to walk to the plantation at Mosquito Inlet as soon as more overseers arrived and provisions were collected, and she wondered how she could get on that list.

She sought out another young Greek woman with whom she'd made friends, and whose features were so similar to her own that they could have been sisters.

"We've been too long at sea, Teresa, and I ache to feel the earth beneath my feet. As far as can be seen, this land is flat, but the city looks much like my home. My heart nearly leapt from me when I heard a crewman shout 'land' and I would gladly swim to shore if I could, but there is to be a march soon, to the doctor's plantation, and I would join it. Would you come with me? Surely the walk couldn't be worse than remaining on this smelly, vermin ridden ship. Walk with me, and we'll make a merry jaunt of it."

Not wanting to disappoint Darian, but neither wishing to go, Teresa pled her own concerns.

"How far might the plantation be? Don't go, Darian, stay here. I have accepted someone, and I've pledged myself to him; I can't go with you now. Our ship does wear a traveler's cloak of stench, but it isn't as pungent on the deck. Stay here with me and Paolo, and we will sail there soon."

"Oh, Paolo is it? He is a handsome man."

"He is endowed with the comely features of the Romans, but he's much more than handsome. He's gentle as well as strong and he has the kindest brown eyes, and his voice," she sighed, "oh, his voice... and he speaks our language!"

"Well then, we will bring him with us and our journey will be all the better for his company. Talk with him, Teresa, and allow the three of us to appeal for a warrant to walk."

With her most entreating smile, Darian then implored,

"We're here, Teresa, we're here! We made it across! Yet we sit on this ship, and I can bear it no longer. Please, Teresa, please come with me."

- - - - -

But any freedom to choose was purely imaginary, for the overseers aboard ship made the assignments for the march, and the passengers were not consulted.

Darian delighted in being among those chosen, but Paolo was also selected, leaving Teresa behind to wait for the ship to be filled with supplies before it resumed its voyage.

Teresa had entered into this venture with reluctance, but her mother had thought it to be her daughter's best chance for survival and her opportunity for a good life. With the relentless persuasion of a desperate and loving mother, she had besieged upon her daughter to go, but knowing that she'd never see her mother or her homeland again had left Teresa feeling empty and deserted.

Melancholy plagued her until Paolo professed his love for her at nearly the end of their voyage, but while Teresa watched the oars lift and dip in unison as her friends were rowed to shore, she felt a wave of loneliness engulf her that seemed as deep as the bay and as dark as the clouds growing in the distance.

2.

Statue still, Maya crouched in the sweltering heat of midday. Salty beads of sweat drizzled over her forehead, stinging her eyes before they splashed onto the bough beneath her chin. Each muscle had stiffened and pleaded for her to move, but the fear of being caught transcended any demands from her small, light brown body.

Her baby lay sleeping on a cloth beside her, quiet for now, but Maya worried that the child would awake at any moment and unknowingly reveal them to the two men who sat conversing on the other side of the giant oak.

She'd come to laze by the river to seek refuge from the scorching temperatures of the oppressively muggy summer day, for some time ago she'd discovered the woven nest of branches where she and her baby hid.

Entwined by nature and feathered in moss, the roost overlooked the water and perched several feet above the ground, but the broad, sprawling arms of the tree offered an easy ascent to what had become her favorite place to get away.

It took only a five minute walk through the jungle-like forest to reach the retreat from her and her husband's cabin, and she'd felt safe there in the past, but overhearing the men, Maya realized her mistake.

How could I be so careless? How could I fall asleep, an' 'low these men came here without my knowin'? Send 'em away Lawd, please, send 'em away!

While the men reclined against the expansive old tree, Maya peered between its branches and the thick, curly tangles of long moss that draped from them. She could see the tops of the men's heads, and her eyes widened as the fairer haired of the two spoke.

"In every town we enter I hear murmurs of war brewing, and this time, Hatcher, the colonists bloody well be rousing it. If we have no wish to be soldiers, we should hie ourselves back to the West."

"War? Bah. There'll be no war. I've heard the rumors, Jonathan, an' everyone likes to complain, but no one will fight the British; they be too rich an' there are too many of 'em, even the Spanish lost to 'em. I have no care whether they hang the king or bow to him; I relish a battle I know I can win. I enjoy crackin' a whip on a slave's back or waitin' in ambush to hear the thump of my club on a skull, but I would greatly dislike shootin' at someone who might return fire."

Maya's limbs railed at her in a high pitched, silent scream. Just when she felt that she could no longer bear the pain of immobility or of hearing another contemptable or cowardly remark, the sandy-haired Jonathan jumped up from his seat.

"You could be right, but let's be on with it. 'Twill take forever if we keep idling about, and I lust to lie in a bed with a woman."

With that, Hatcher's demeanor changed from thoughtfully serious to a crooked smirk.

"If you be thinkin' of a wench's company this night, you best think again; we'll not be seein' Saint Augustine till tomorrow."

Jonathan laughed, "'Twill be longer than that if we don't get to the road. This be a pleasant scene and 'twas a welcome rest, but we'll earn no money here nor nuzzle in a soft, flowery scented bosom."

Instead of rising, Hatcher slumped a little lower, and Jonathan nudged him with the crusty toe of his boot.

"Get up, we need be on our way. We've drunk the dregs of our ale, and the horses have had their fill of that foul tasting river."

While the men bundled their gear and readied their

9

horses, Maya's son stirred and gurgled, then contorted his face as he began a fretful cry. Maya took him quickly to her breast, and prayed that the men hadn't heard the sound or noticed her movement, but Hatcher stopped and cocked his head.

"Did you hear that, Jonathan? I heard somethin'."

Maya tried to be calm, but she barely dared to breathe as she muffled the baby's suckling sounds with her chemise which, soaked in perspiration, clung to her.

She'd hidden from bounty hunters before, but two years had passed since that terror. She'd become forgetful of the danger, and never had the stakes been so high.

Dear Lawd, foh the baby's sake, make 'em leave!

For a moment, Jonathan stood motionless to listen, then he shook his head and shrugged.

"No, I hear nothing."

"It sounded like an infant's cry."

"A cat perhaps."

"Nah, a cat's yowl would have stirred the horses."

"A bird then."

Hatcher gazed up and searched into the tree.

"Might have been, but if slaves be about, we could fatten our purse an' buy whores in the best tavern of the city."

A scowl formed across Jonathan's face.

"We hold ample silver in our pocket for women, but if anyone be about, more than likely it be Indians, and

I have no wish to fight Indians. We should carry on, business awaits us."

Hatcher coughed and spit on the ground, and as he exaggerated the labor it took to mount his horse, he griped,

"How does a man work in this stiflin' air? 'Tis a bloody chore just to straddle my horse. If good positions had not been ensured for us, I might be decidin' the West be agreeable an' we would become common pioneers again. Aah, but to be overseers at a plantation, now that be a more befittin' profession. We'll reap a handsome wage, an' I will still have the occasion to rap on some heads."

As they began to saunter away, their horses following a narrow deer path into the dense brush and scrub palms, Maya drew in a much needed breath, but in that sigh her baby finished draining the breast he nursed upon.

She moved him to the other teat and encouraged him to continue, but a short wail escaped before the infant settled into the new arrangement, and Maya's heart sank with horror.

Halting the horses, Hatcher shifted in his saddle to look back.

"I heard it again just now. That be no bloody bird."

Without a moment for caution, and while the tree and undergrowth shielded her from their view, Maya swiftly wrapped the cloth and baby tightly around herself. Hunching down, she ran agilely along a

11

sizeable branch in the opposite direction of the men.

When she leapt from the tree, a bush softened her landing and a young doe that had secluded itself in a den of leaves behind it took flight. The startled animal ran crashing through the woods toward the men, convincing them that the noises Maya and her baby had made came from the doe.

Hatcher whispered as he reached for his rifle,

"See there, a fine supper for us!"

Jonathan thrust out his arm to stop him.

"We have no time for dressing game. Leave it be and we'll roast her fawn on another day."

Excited by the prospect of a kill, Hatcher could not be dissuaded. A bullet burst from its chamber with a resounding blast, but the projectile missed its mark, and the doe ran on.

Concealed in the bushes, Maya cradled her son close as burning fire ate like acid into her back and blood seeped through her wet chemise. She gritted her teeth to keep from crying out while she made sure that her baby was unharmed, and as tears of pain and fear for her child welled up in her frightened eyes, the two men rode away.

- - - - -

The report of a gun's fire echoed through the surrounding trees as Rafe prepared a section of his garden for seed. The sound seemed to originate by the river, and at first, he thought someone from the Native village nearby was hunting for deer, then he remembered.

Maya and Eli! They're at the river!

The hairs on the nape of his neck prickled as he threw down his one man plow and took off running toward the spot.

A stone's throw away, at the home of Noah and Ruth, the shot shattered the serenity of the forest, and the disturbance brought Noah out onto his front porch.

He saw Rafe running toward the path to the river and he called to him, but when Rafe disappeared into the woods without a reply, Noah sprang to follow him.

As Rafe sped down the snaking trail, his fears for Maya and the baby distracted him from taking care for his own safety, and without being aware of it, he ran within the scope of vision of two men on horseback.

He stopped too late to hide when he saw them, and the gun aimed at him persuaded him to be obedient, but he protested.

"I am a freeman an' I live among Natives. Leave me be an' no harm will come to you."

The man holding the gun laughed and asked his companion,

"Did you hear somethin' Jonathan? I think this arrogant lump tried to speak."

In a trice, Rafe was being towed on his way for an anxiety fraught, fast trot to St. Augustine, with his wrists bound together and a tether tied around his waist.

When Noah heard a man barking orders he hid in a cluster of palms in time to avoid being seen, but as he spied from behind the fronds, he saw a gun and watched as two men tied Rafe in rope and pulled him away.

Fearing that both he and Rafe would be taken or shot if he rushed out to try to rescue his friend, Noah waited for the men to ride out of sight, but when he headed toward the village to get help, he heard the faint cries of a baby.

Eli! An' it sho Maya be with him. Rafe mustah been runnin' tah 'em. Deah Lawd, what hell is this? Ain't nothin' I can do foh Rafe till I know they be safe.

When Noah reached Maya and Eli, he fell to his knees beside them.

Curled around her son and on the edge of unconsciousness, Maya murmured,

"Take the baby. I been shot."

Noah's heart wrenched with pain and sympathy.

"I take you both Maya, don' you worry. I git Eli an' you home. I git you home an' I git the medicine doctah an' he make you well, Maya, I sweah. I sling Eli 'round me an' I throw you ovah my shouldah an' we be home in no time. Everahthin' gonna be fine, an' Ruth gonna take good care o' you, don' you worry."

Bent over, but with good speed, considering the root filled path, Noah carried the two of them as if they weighed no more than a shirt. He thought that Maya would all too soon bear more of a burden than he did himself and he put off telling her of Rafe's capture.

- - - - -

While Hatcher and Jonathan rode on their way to St. Augustine, they amused themselves with raillery and talked as if Rafe didn't exist, for to them he was nothing more than a commodity.

Whenever Rafe slowed down from fatigue or willfulness, Hatcher would goad him with his whip, or drag him after a vicious yank on the rope.

Rafe strained to persevere, but a terrible dread that his wife or child could be dead came over him, and bitter memories of his and Maya's former enslavement by an abusive master churned in him.

His stomach roiled with every running stride, but when his captors joked about the doe that Hatcher's bullet had missed, he came to believe with some relief that they had no knowledge of Maya or Eli, and he began to consider St. Augustine as a fortunate destination.

I can tell by their talk that these men don't know the city, but I do. I have friends there, an' Ben an' Rose or Sam might help me.

With a few hours of travel yet ahead of them, they made camp at nightfall near the bank of a small stream where it trickled out from a murky cypress swamp.

Jonathan reached into a sack and grabbed a chunk of salt pork, which he shared with Hatcher, then he gave a slice of the dried meat and a scrap of hard biscuit to

Rafe, and allowed him to drink from the black water stream.

It was more than Rafe expected and he was thankful for it, but Jonathan's consideration met with Hatcher's disapproval.

For the assurance that their slave wouldn't flee in the night, and for his own and Jonathan's safe and uninterrupted sleep, Hatcher trussed Rafe to a tree.

3.

Letticia McGinn had a temper as searing as the Florida sun in July, and when the temperature rose, her anger could boil up quick as an afternoon thunder cloud, then steam like the rising vapor after the rain had passed.

Her husband, and many of the townsfolk, made efforts to stay out of her way, but her nearest neighbors found her impossible to avoid.

When Ben and Rose Stewart moved to St. Augustine from Charles Town, they purchased the modest estate next to the McGinn's. A bargain, they thought at the time.

Influenced by other British Colonists who were also new to the city, they removed the Spanish style coquina from the exterior of their home and tore down its surrounding coquina wall, to alter the house into a closer resemblance of their own British, clapboard architecture.

They learned too late that the shell rock and mortar would have helped to reduce the baking heat of summer inside, and the wall could have extended them some privacy from Letticia, as well as years of her impertinent meddling.

A hot, humid evening brought the Stewarts out onto their front stoop to savor the cooler air, but as they watched the fading hues of a once vivid sunset, an unwelcome appearance intruded into their view.

Rose sat upright, straightened her shoulders, and patted Ben's knee.

"Here comes Lettie. What could she be wanting of us now?"

As Ben turned to look, he grunted his dismay.

"The woman never sleeps. Has she not the decency to keep to her own property at night?"

Perceiving herself to be captain of the quarter, Lettie barged up the lane toward them, creating a wide wake of self-importance as she trawled the sand with the back hems of her voluminous skirts.

With affected sweetness, she addressed Ben,

"Good evening to you Mister Stewart."

Then, with a not so hidden sting of brine in her voice,

"Good evening, Mistress Stewart."

Rose gave a half-hearted smile with her greeting, but Ben's voice did not disguise his mild annoyance.

"Good even', Mistress McGinn. What pressing affair brings you to our home this evening?"

In the condescending posture which she often assumed, Lettie lifted her nose as she spoke to them.

"I believe the news my Angus heard at the public house will be of interest to you."

Then she paused to hold their attention and slid her tongue across her lips as if the information and the moment tasted delicious.

"Another shipload of indentured servants moors in the harbor, and like the last pack of them, they be laden with misery and on a course south to that Mosquito Inlet of Doctor Turnbull's."

Crumpling her nose and skewing her mouth, she glowered at Ben and Rose with fierce intensity.

"They call them Menorcans, but I know they are Spanish. 'Tis said they have few houses and little food to eat. Hah! Be sure, they get what they deserve! The Spanish burned and ravaged this town when they left, now this word spreads like fire through the city – the doctor will pay for dry goods and food for his servants. If you have any cloth, Rose, you would do well to sell it now. We can make a pretty penny off the sorry lot of them. Know that I shall give the price of milk from my cow a rise, for it be not swill milk; I do not feed her beer."

Ben shook his head in exasperation.

"I don't believe that all of the doctor's indentured servants are Spanish, but where they came from should be of no matter, and none of them ever lived in our city. You must recall, Letticia, 'twas not so long ago we too sailed on ships to colonize. We were fortunate to be given help from others then, and you can never know when we may need help again."

Quick to seethe at Ben's admonishment, Lettie's round face turned cherry red as she reached her exploding point.

"Would you have me give them the milk then? Why, they are nothing more than slaves! I shall pocket a tidy sum from their wealthy owner, and mind you, you might do the same!"

Rose could hold her tongue no longer.

"Make your gain, Letticia, but there be no need to extort the man; the poor settlers shall be the ones to have the less for it."

Flaring her nostrils and narrowing her eyes, Lettie gathered her skirts in front of her, and with an indignant and audible huff, she launched herself down the lane back to her house while the last of dusk drifted into darkness.

As he watched the dramatic performance, Ben shook his head again and moaned to Rose.

"She is our neighbor, and by our faith I must love her,

but the woman makes that a herculean feat. I hadn't the chance to tell what I have heard. 'Tis said at the dock that Turnbull owes everyone, for he pays with notes, and the merchants have yet to see the silver."

Rose raised her brow. "Be the doctor not a Scotsman, as are we? What choice have we but to give him our trust? We have a measure of cloth, one which I wove to give to Maya and Rafe, but I can weave another, and we could put a few coins to good use on this land. If we are never paid, then we shall abide with it, but we shall not turn away from people in need."

4.

The sun hadn't neared its highest point when Hatcher, Jonathan, and their tethered captive, Rafe, arrived in St. Augustine, but the heat already broiled.

The hot woolen uniform worn by the sentry at the city gate had put him in an ill humor, and he angrily shouted orders to the two riders.

"Sirs, dismount your horses!"

As he inspected their prisoner, he demanded, "What have you here?"

Hatcher exchanged a furtive glance with Jonathan, and waved his hat to cool himself as he answered.

"My dear sir, we came upon this runaway in the woods a day ago. We do our duty to our sovereign king an' a service to his owner to return him."

The guard then peered at Rafe.

"And what say you?"

Covered in a skin of mud made from his sweat and dirt from the road, Rafe stood his tallest and firmly opposed his captors.

"Sir, I told them I am a freeman, but the clink of coins be all they want to hear."

Hatcher quickly took the offensive.

"Do not believe a word! Why would you ask this insignificant grub to speak? He has no paper. He's a bloody runaway!"

Irritated by Hatcher's insolent disposition and the incessant fanning of his hat, the guard snatched the hat from Hatcher's hand and flung it.

"Enough! I know this man. His name is Rafe, and I know him to be a freed man. I have purchased furniture that he makes and brings here to sell. Untie him or be bound in rope yourselves."

Jonathan removed his own hat and made a short bow to the guard as he attempted to ease the stress of the situation.

"Sir, we beg your pardon and ask for your clemency. A Doctor Turnbull has commissioned us to be overseers and we are to meet a ship of his here. Please understand our plight in the forest for we had no way of knowing that this person spoke the truth. 'Tis our experience that any slave will lie, and we merely cared to do the right thing by our king."

Although Jonathan's logic softened the guard to some degree, he didn't seem entirely convinced as he squinted an eye.

"By my experience, most men will lie to save their life, but then, only a fool would not. Let this man go and be on with your business, and see to it that you behave as gentlemen in this city."

Hatcher retrieved his hat and whopped it on his thigh to shake the sand and dirt from it, and as he mumbled his discontent, he mocked himself.

"'Our duty to our sovereign king'. What bloody drivel – an' the dunce believed it! Yet he deprived us of our bounty. Were I a younger man, I would have the dolt's head."

While they walked their horses into town, Hatcher continued to mutter his rant, but before they headed to the landing to seek Dr. Turnbull, they entered the first public house they came upon.

Beneath the wide beams and low ceiling of a stale and musty room, Jonathan sat down at a long plank table and brooded quietly, for he'd found only drink and disappointment as the one woman there was the barmaid, whom he thought to be rather old and unattractive for his taste.

At the other end of the table, Hatcher indulged a garrulous fellow who gladly helped him to guzzle a pitcher of beer.

"Angus, my friend, the sentries of this city be a querulous lot, an' stand not for fine citizens such as ourselves. When my partner an' I entered the city this morn, a bloody guard denied our claim to the runaway we'd caught in the woods, an' he insisted on the release of him. 'Twas a beastly greetin' an' a nasty bite from our silver, but that be not the worst of it; the infernal gatekeeper disgraced me in front of the filthy wretch!"

Not wishing to offend the man who'd paid for his drinks, Angus sympathized.

"Aye, I could tell you stories about my wife's quarrels with the authorities, for they have treated the woman harshly, as they have you, sir."

While he reflected on those incidents, an image of his wife, red-faced, spewing spit and shaking her fist at the constable came to mind, and he chuckled heartily.

"Ah, but in her case, they were likely right! Constable Grimes believes she be unhinged, and 'tis the kindest word he says of her! Letticia is..."

Angus lowered his voice and leaned in toward Hatcher, even though Letticia wasn't there.

"a mean, spiteful shrew! I spend time in the taverns to evade her! 'Twere na' that the woman can cook I'd ne'er go home, but by my word, every meal she makes tastes good as a king's banquet. You would be welcome to partake of dinner at my home today, and save me from the awful fate of being alone with her!"

Angus's humorous predicament effectively altered Hatcher's mood, and Hatcher roared with laughter.

26

"Ha! Fishwives an' viragoes be the very reason that I am not married! My belly will indeed be disappointed at the loss of a meal as tasty as you describe, but I am obliged to meet with a ship of Doctor Turnbull's."

"Doctor Turnbull! The air is full with talk of him. Many in town dislike having his Menorcans settle south of here, though the same seem anxious to sell the doctor anything that will sustain them. My wife hisses like a cat at the mention of the word, and she disparages our neighbors for their willingness to be charitable t'ward them, but Lettie be ready and eager to profit by them. For myself, as long as they leave me my drink, I care na' one whit nor t'other."

- - - - -

Rafe considered it to be beyond luck that he knew the commanding guard on duty, and at his release, he swore,

"I will bring you two of the most comfortable chairs you evah sat on."

Weary and sore, he set out for the long journey home, but in a few minutes, a small party of men from his village met up with him.

Although they had arrived too late to carry out a rescue, Rafe appreciated their intentions and that there had been no need for violence. His friends' protection and a ride home on the horse they'd brought for him were gratefully accepted.

On learning of Maya's injury, he howled a loud and

anguished plea to the heavens and urged the men to quicken their horses. To himself, Rafe couldn't help but regret that the two mercenaries hadn't encountered a painful end.

5.

It took a day for the Native doctor to be brought from another village where he'd gone to trade for herbs and medicines, and with the delay, Noah feared the worst for Maya, but Ruth kept a hopeful vigil.

The quiet mannered, yet powerful of spirit and highly respected medicine man spoke several languages, and was considered by many to be better at the art of healing than any of the white doctors in the area.

While he administered to Maya inside of Ruth and Noah's cabin, Ruth paced restlessly outside as she nestled Maya's baby in her arms.

Moving to the rhythm of the healer's ceremonial chants, Noah picked an armful of vegetables, collected some eggs, and chose from his shed several strips of jerked deer meat. He stuffed everything into a large basket, added a few rabbit pelts and a carpentry tool that he'd made, then wandered about his garden while he worried and waited.

- - - - -

A year older than Ruth, Noah's noble heart was nearly as big as his tall, muscular body. He'd vowed to always protect Ruth and do anything for her, and although he did his best to honor those promises, Ruth's desire to bear his child had gone unfulfilled.

As he watched her cuddle Eli, his distress over that omission emerged anew, adding to the despair he felt over Maya and Rafe.

Ruth and Maya had become friends five years previous, during their enslavement on a plantation in Carolina where Noah had also served as a slave.

When Ruth arrived, purchased from a neighboring estate, Noah moved quickly to lift her down from the master's cart. As he clasped her slender waist between his large, calloused hands, they both felt the overpowering thrill of love at first sight.

Fourteen years of age at that time, Ruth bore an angular, though angelic face, and a sturdy, yet lithe figure. A life of oppression had taught her to be shy, but she possessed a natural talent for singing and an

30

appealing ability to be optimistic.

Born into slavery in the Colonies, she hadn't received a formal education, but she'd seen enough to be aware of the perils of her station.

In order to prevent Ruth from becoming an unwilling victim of their licentious master, and to rescue Maya from being subjected to any more assaults by him, the three young people made a daring escape along with two other, older friends, Sary and Lucas.

They had hoped to reach the Spanish fort, Fort Mose at St. Augustine where they believed they could obtain freedom, and where they'd heard Rafe resided after their master separated him from Maya and sent him away to be sold.

Tragically, Sary and Lucas did not survive the nearly two years of ordeals which they suffered in the undertaking. Sary succumbed to an illness that Ruth thought to be caused by spoiled food, and Lucas drowned when one of their primitive ferries overturned in the onslaught of a flood. A flood which nearly drowned them all.

Almost to their goal of Fort Mose, one of their camps in the woods was discovered and brutally raided by two bounty hunters, but while Ruth and Noah were chased through the woods by one of them, the other hunter captured Maya and took her in chains to St. Augustine.

By then, Great Britain had acquired the city from the Spanish, and the Spanish had sailed from St. Augustine to resettle in Cuba.

The freed slaves living in Fort Mose had gone with the Spanish, along with the potential of freedom for other escaped slaves.

With the help of Ben and Rose in St. Augustine, Maya escaped her captor, and also with their help, she was reunited with Rafe and her friends Ruth and Noah at Rafe's cabin.

Unfortunately, by a twist of fate, the same mercenaries who had invaded their camp came upon them at that cabin, and reigned in terror over them.

Ruth had garnered inner strength and purpose through her endurance of those horrible events, but much of her fortitude could be attributed to the love she found with Noah and the devoted friendship which had forged between herself and Maya.

- - - - -

When the Native doctor finished tending to Maya, he packed his herbs and sacred implements into deer hide pouches then came out onto the small porch.

Eager to hear his news, Ruth stopped abruptly when she saw him.

"Maya will recovah?"

"There is hope, but the bullet remains."

His answer shocked both Ruth and Noah, but Ruth boldly confronted him.

"Why? Why ain't it out?"

"Too dangerous to remove."

"Oh Lawd! Maya... deah Lawd. You have medicine we can give her?"

"I have used what I have. If there comes a need, I will return."

Ruth felt too frustrated to let it go.

"Ain't theah something we can do foh her? Theah must be something."

"Take her son to her."

Noah had patiently waited his turn, and as he lowered his head in somber resignation, he handed the filled basket to the doctor.

"I will bring you mo'."

The doctor curled his lips into a reserved, but compassionate smile.

"This is enough."

"Is theah anythin' we can do foh you?"

"I will think on that and let you know."

As the doctor stepped down from the stoop to leave, he placed his hand on Noah's shoulder, lightly, but with great caring.

"If she has courage, and the desire to live, she has an able chance."

The tension in Noah's shoulders eased, and he inhaled deeply, as though he'd been forgetting to breathe.

"I nevah knowed a body bravah 'n Maya, oh mo' wantin' tah live, even when she was willin' tah die at the hands o' bounty huntahs tah save her friends."

6.

In the hope of avoiding much of the torrid heat of day, Sam Coxe started out for St. Augustine by the light of a thin ribbon of dawn.

With his wagon emptied and no need for hurry, he gave his horse Amelia free rein, and enabled to choose her own pace, she favored a happy speed for she knew that the trail from Fort Picolata led home.

Although Sam valued his job and the time he spent on the road with Amelia making deliveries from St. Augustine, after he'd unloaded the supplies and submitted himself to the rustic overnight lodgings of the ground outside the fort, he looked forward to spending the coming night at home in his comfortable bed with his Native wife Eyota.

- - - - -

Sam and Eyota had wed at Eyota's small, peaceful village, in a stunning and touching ceremony beside a beautiful cove of a river called Welaka by the Natives, but named St. Johns by the British.

Ben and Rose, Rafe and Maya, and Noah and Ruth were among those attending, and when Sam and Eyota slipped away after the wedding, their friends continued to celebrate through the night with a sumptuous feast.

The newly married couple enjoyed a week of privacy in Eyota's frond thatched cabin, before they moved to St. Augustine, where Sam owned a home and operated his delivery service.

Their union was mostly accepted by the city's populace, but on occasion, Eyota suffered the bitter tongues of jealous women who spouted spiteful remarks just loud enough to be heard.

There were a few of either gender who would, at times, exhibit their loutish behavior to both Sam and Eyota, but Eyota had an intelligent mind and a strong heart. Firm in her love and in her abilities (she was known for the beauty of her functional pottery), she overlooked their churlishness for Sam, and earned the friendships of kinder residents.

- - - - -

Five hours into the normally six hour return trip to St. Augustine, Sam was falling in and out of sleep when Amelia skipped and whinnied then came to a halt, jostling Sam fully awake.

Startled by the stop, and seeing a small band of men rapidly approaching on horseback, Sam readied his pistol, but as the men rode closer he could see that his friend Rafe was one of them.

Not waiting for an exchange of greetings, Rafe spurted out,

"Sam! Bounty huntahs shot Maya! The doctah is sent for, an' I rush to be with her. The huntahs – their names be Hatchah an' Jonathan – tied me in rope an' dragged me through hell to Saint Augustine where a guard I know freed me. I have no time to say more, but Maya would want Mistah Ben and Miz Rose to know."

"Dear God, Rafe, this is terrible news. I will tell them and we will come, but should those mercenary scum cross my path, be sure, I'll have them pleading for mercy at the muzzle of my gun."

While he watched the riders gallop away, Sam noticed that heavy clouds to the west were expanding toward him, and he spoke to his horse.

"You heard as well as I, Amelia, we have no time for delay."

Amelia seemed to understand (which did not surprise Sam for they had lived and worked together for years), and before he could flick her reins, she ran on with a brisk gait.

Even though Sam supposed she couldn't hear him over the noise of the bumping wagon, he shared his thoughts with her, as he often did.

"Amelia, my girl, would that you could talk, for I have no wish to bring good friends such dire tidings. Maya has come to be a daughter to Ben and Rose, and they have mourned the loss of too many children, but there be no task that I would not do for Rafe. 'Twas he who acquainted me with my lovely Eyota. Do you remember the day a bounty hunting maggot destroyed our wagon in his attempt to strangle me? Rafe saved my life, and yes Amelia, I believe he also saved yours."

7.

Accustomed to the rolling undulations of the sea, Darian's legs wobbled then gave way from under her as she took her first steps on land in the New World – land beneath two feet of water in the harbor of St. Augustine.

Buoyant with trapped air, her skirt billowed up around her, and flailing her arms about, she playfully bashed at the floating pillows of cloth while she took advantage of the opportunity to clean and cool herself.

She joyfully grabbed up a handful of wet sand.

A new land! A new life! I am here!

As the sand oozed between her fingers, she felt what seemed to be a piece of shell, but when she examined the fragment, she was amazed to see a small, Spanish silver coin.

A coin! This land has bestowed riches upon me! A wonderful omen!

She tucked the coin into the pocket she wore underneath her skirt and excitedly scooped the sand again, but she found nothing, and an overseer yelled at her to get up.

When she reached for the hand offered to her in help, she looked up into the smiling face of Paolo.

Teresa is right, Paolo does have the kindest brown eyes, but I will tell no one about the coin, not him, not even Teresa.

"Thank you, Paolo, I must learn to walk on land again."

Paolo's smile broadened to a grin.

"Until then, I am your servant."

Soaked with seawater, her clothes dripped a stream as she steadied herself on shore, and when she lifted her skirt to wring it out, she displayed a pair of shapely legs.

The outline of her youthful round breasts showed clearly through her wet bodice, but she had long before given up any vestiges of modesty, for the packed ship had afforded little privacy.

While Paolo admired the presentation, another handsome young man at the landing also watched her with enthusiasm.

Sitting on his horse, Jonathan stared at Darian, while Hatcher badgered the servants into a manageable file to march behind the supply wagon.

When Darian noticed her audience, she smiled and smoothed her clothing in a fun-loving, but brazen, tease.

Hatcher wasn't pleased, and he snapped his whip to get their attention.

"Jonathan! Get to work. I have no use for a gapin' schoolboy. Woman, get in the line. I'll brook no trouble from the likes of you."

With another loud clap, the tip of Hatcher's whip licked the wet hem of Darian's skirt. She flinched at the sound and its slice, and at the flash of malice she saw in Hatcher's eyes.

Hatcher felt no need to hide his disdain.

"'Tis a far way to Mosquito Inlet. I can make the journey very painful for you."

His tone was obvious, and the meaning of his words clear. She took a place among the other servants as she wondered in fear.

What have I gotten myself into? My Lord, protect me.

8.

Intent in his errand, the wait to enter the city at its gate aggravated Sam, but once inside the wall, the rows of indentured servants at the landing caught his interest.

When he saw an overseer lash a whip towards a pretty young woman, he bristled with anger. Although her skirt was slashed, she wasn't harmed, but he felt sorry for her.

Thinking that he might cause her more trouble if he interfered, he hurried Amelia onward while he pondered over his own problems.

Leaving his wagon on the lane in front of his house, Sam cried out for his wife as he pulled the front door open. This wasn't his usual homecoming, and although Eyota came quickly, Sam had already begun to gather items for their trip.

"I met Rafe on the road. Bounty hunters have shot Maya. He asked me to tell Ben and Rose."

"Does she live?"

"Rafe believes she is alive, and the doctor is with her. We need to pack for a journey to the village, and we'll stop at the Stewart's on our way."

- - - - -

Rose wanted to be on the road as soon as she heard the story from Sam, but after a thoughtful moment she asked,

"You say the men be called Hatcher and Jonathan? Surely the man named Jonathan is not my son, but Jonathan be the name of our youngest son. He and two of his brothers left us to pioneer the West some years ago. The not knowing where our sons may be, or if they are well or hurt or hungry or whether they be still alive, gnaws at my heart, but I shall always pray for my children and wish for them to be with me. I pray that Maya shall not also be lost to us."

Ben missed his offspring and feared for Maya almost as much as Rose, but he made an effort to sooth her.

"All shall be well, Rose. The doctor will have attended her, and when we arrive she shall chide us for our worries. Ready food and blankets for our journey while I harness Henry. Come ride with us, Sam, you and Eyota. Amelia must be tired, and Henry can draw us all with good speed."

"'Tis a kind invitation, but I cannot abandon Amelia." Rose would not allow dissent.

"Certainly not. Tie Amelia to our wagon. She shall have no need to draft, yet she shall be with us."

Sam started to head for the barn with Ben, but he stopped and frowned as he remembered.

"Gray clouds hang between us and the village, and the day is near noon, perhaps 'twould be best to wait for tomorrow."

Rose was aghast. "Sampson Coxe! Be on with you! Ben has an oiled canvas we shall use to keep dry if need be. No wee bit of rain nor moonless night shall stay me from Maya. 'Twill take us all of a day and a half, and the half shall be today."

- - - - -

Liberated at last from the ship onto the solid ground of the New World, an excited chatter of speculation arose through the line of immigrants as they filed through the city gate to begin their march to Doctor Turnbull's plantation, but as they proceeded, their militant overseers commanded them to be silent and walk faster.

Waiting as patiently as they were able for the line to pass, Ben and Sam sat on the high front seat of Ben's wagon while Rose and Eyota sat facing the other way on a small bench in the box behind them, but when one of the overseers scored a man's skin with his whip, it was hard for Sam to remain seated.

"I saw that cur use his whip to threaten a young woman at the landing. These poor people are bound for more misery than they bargained for."

On the other side of the road, another overseer hollered, "Hatcher! Over here!" and the man with the whip turned his horse around.

Sam reached for his gun.

"If not for the sentries at the gate, I would shoot that swine dead."

Rose twisted to look and turned bloodless pale. Torn between love and loathing, she sat frozen while she stared at the man on horseback who had called for Hatcher.

Ben felt as if he'd fallen into a hole, and he haltingly whispered,

"Jonathan... our son."

Finding her voice, Rose echoed Ben's words softly, "Jonathan, our son."

Then louder, with a vehemence unlike her, she spat, "Jonathan our son!"

Hearing his name, Jonathan looked across the road to Ben and Rose. In that moment of recognition he forgot his job, his place, and his partner, everything except his parents.

He leapt from his horse and ran to them hailing,

"Mother! Father!"

In a steeled pose, with her arms folded sternly in front of her, Rose stood above him in the wagon.

"I see a face much the same as that of my son, but you cannot be my son."

Puzzled by her coldness, Jonathan held out his arms.

"Mother, 'tis I, Jonathan, your son. Father, I am your son."

Rose fought her feelings of yearning for him and held steadfast.

"I reared no son to be a brutish overseer or murderous mercenary. My son Jonathan be a kind and loving young man who went to the West. No, you cannot be my son."

"Mother, I am he. I have come here to be an overseer, but I am not unfeeling and I am no murderer. Why would you say these things to me?"

Ben stroked Rose's arm to calm her, and with the touch, sorted through his own torment.

God, help me, what shall I do? Do I hug him? Or do I strike him? He is our son. A child of our blood. We haven't seen him in years. How can I deny him... but how can I not?

"I shall speak with the lad, Rose."

Distressed by the awkward circumstance, but having sympathy for Rose, Sam glared as he and Eyota sat quietly while Ben hopped down from the wagon and drew Jonathan aside.

"Can you give news of your brothers to your

mother?"

"Only that I parted ways with William and Aaron four years ago when we left the Ohio Territory. They set off for Philadelphia, and I to Charles Town."

Ben rubbed a finger on his lips and tapped the dirt with his foot, for he dreaded to hear the answers his next questions might bring.

"We have been told that bounty hunters, by the names of Hatcher and Jonathan, shot a woman who is as dear to us as a daughter. We go to her now, and your mother is beside herself with worry that she will have died."

"Father, I swear to you, I have shot no one, nor have I knowledge of anyone shot by Mister Hatcher. I've traveled with him for some months, and the man is coarse and ill mannered, but he be no murderer."

"Be you bounty hunters? Did you restrain a man then drag him here to sell for a reward?"

Jonathan hung his head and said nothing.

Ben knew what that meant.

"When all of our flesh and blood be gone from us, the man you took be a son to us, a good man, with a son of his own. We know that you live, 'twill be enough, for your mother and I shall not entertain bounty hunters. See to your horse and your job."

As Ben walked back to Rose he wiped the beads of sweat from his brow and dabbed at his eyes. In the strain of his anguish, he thought the world, and himself, to be cruel.

Jonathan went over to a guard and pointed to the wagon.

"Sir, the citizens there be on an urgent mission to a dying woman and are in need of swift passage. Do you know these people? If you can let them through, I will shift the line of marchers to the side."

He slipped the only two coins he had into the guard's hand, and the man smiled slyly, with satisfaction, as he closed his fist around them.

"I know them. They live in town. The men pass here to make their deliveries from the ships, and now and again their wives be with them. You sir, are also known to me, to my displeasure. Nevertheless, I will send them through."

When the guard waved them on, Rose began to weep,

"Dear Lord, forgive me. I do love him, yet I cannot find it in me to like him."

Ben had seen what Rose had not, and he tried to comfort her.

"There appears to be some good in him Rose, perhaps that part comes from you."

9.

While Darian walked down the narrow road to Mosquito Inlet, her few possessions, other than the clothes she wore, were slung across her body in a large cloth bag.

The half-filled bag and the cloak that she'd thrown over her shoulder had fallen into the harbor with her, and for a time she welcomed the cooling wetness of her attire and her baggage, but their weight added to the struggle of her passage and her wet shoes rubbed sores into her feet.

She'd almost forgotten her pain, her doubts, and her

fear of the overseers as she marveled at the lush, yet strange and mysterious landscapes around her.

Massive trees seemed to spawn the delicate ferns which adorned them, and the lengthy tresses of moss that dangled from their gnarled branches enchanted her.

The black water creeks edged with wide spears of green leaves appeared mystical in their stillness, and the swamps, although oddly menacing, had a compelling, magical beauty of their own.

The road was little more than a winding path of sand strewn randomly with broken shells, and less than that in several places where foliage had taken over.

Largely, the pathway made use of old trails that had been blazed through the woods by Natives to avoid the deeper places of swamps and streams, but watery crossings were many, and the marchers often walked in a state of wetness.

Softened by the long voyage, their feet were either blistered by their shoes or, if they chose to walk unshod, cut by the shells and brambles of the path.

Where bridges existed they were no more than a few roughly hewn logs, and the dangerous jobs of getting the wagon over the timbers went to the men walking near it, but the majesty of the scenery fostered Darian's resolve, and she spoke to Paolo of her hopes for owning her own farm in the future while she walked beside him.

Many of the settlers walked in single file, which the

overseers preferred, for that deterred conversation, but the scattered length of the line also made the policing of it inconvenient. Hatcher held a position in the rear while Jonathan rode to the side of the center, and the wagon driver, the towering John Taggart, led the way with his comparatively diminutive assistant.

If a marcher's movements could be interpreted as an attempt to flee, Hatcher seemed pleased to use his power to thwart the possibility, and stragglers were vulnerable to his abuse.

In the late afternoon, when Darian sat down on a fallen tree trunk by the side of the road to remove her torturous shoes, she received the full force of Hatcher's long whip.

Coming to her aid, Paolo tried to grab the thong of the whip, but Hatcher thrashed Paolo in a fury and reared up his horse as he attacked. Wild eyed and snorting, the steed looked to be sharing in his owner's lurid enjoyment.

At the sound of a woman's scream, Jonathan quickly wound his way back along the trail to find Paolo on his knees, bloodied, with his shirt in tatters.

Angered, Jonathan demanded, "What has this man done?"

Hatcher gestured toward Darian.

"I caught the bloody sneak tryin' to run into the woods with that woman."

Afraid, but appalled, Darian mustered her strength and defied him.

53

"He lies! It's a lie! I take my shoes from my sore feet and he whip me. Paolo save me."

A man who had followed Paolo and Darian in line also found the courage to speak.

"She tells the truth! I saw it. Look, her feet, they are bare, and her shoes, there."

Hatcher raised his whip in a threat.

"Silence! Or be next!"

Then he sidled his horse up to Jonathan's, and with an appearance of talking privately he spoke loudly, to insure that he would be heard by any marchers close to him.

"They were set to run. I'm sure of it. Do not trust these indents, Jonathan. Better to flay 'em to death 'n chase 'em through a swamp, for a man might fear a whip, while the bloody alligators will not, an' I'll not risk my life nor my horse's for a worthless slave."

Jonathan looked up to the clouds and felt lowly beneath them as he searched for something more than the weather.

What have I become? A man like him? A callous, hardened monster who feels merely scorn and hatred? I have never thought that of myself, but if I stand aside as he cruelly maims or murders, am I not then as guilty as he? Am I the man my mother believes me to be? God help me. My mother deserves a better son.

Disappointed with himself, he dismissed Hatcher.

"We have traveled for hours, and the sun is soon down. This man will need rest if he is to walk tomorrow's long march. I saw a field ahead that would make a good encampment. Ride up and stop the wagon. Gather the marchers. You and John Taggart must be as hungry as I. We shall have our supper and take turns for the night watch."

Annoyed, Hatcher sneered, "Ah now, so you think you can be orderin' me about?"

Jonathan ignored the derision. "Are we not partners? Don't waste what light remains in an argument. I'll keep an eye on these people and get them to the wagon."

"Your eye be on none other 'n that tripe. Beware, Jonathan, don't be trapped in her snare; a woman like that will ruin your life. You would do better to buy a whore's service in town."

With a dig of his heels, Hatcher spurred his horse on and rode to the front of the line, while Jonathan dismounted his own horse and walked directly to Darian.

"We camp ahead, and you and your friend will have the night to heal. I am not like Hatcher and I won't let him hurt you again. My name is Jonathan. What is your name?"

Even though she didn't understand all of his words, Darian felt her body fill with a tingling surge of excitement at his interest. Self-assured, but without pretension, she met his eyes warmly with her own.

"My name is Darian."

10.

The canopy of the forest provided little sanctuary when a blustering storm teemed down on Rafe and his Native companions as they rode from St. Augustine back to their village, and after a rest under the boughs they traveled on through the deluge.

Wet and tired, they arrived at Noah and Ruth's cabin at twilight, and although the rain had stopped, lightning still flickered in distant purple clouds and the rumbling of thunder could be heard.

Relieved and thankful at Rafe's homecoming, Ruth offered soup to everyone and dry clothes to Rafe, but the village men rode on to their homes, and Rafe could think only of seeing Maya.

Ruth began to tell him about everything that had happened while he'd been away, but Rafe hardly heard a word as he went to his wife.

A candle's low light softly lit the tiny room where Maya lay sleeping with her baby, and Rafe kissed her forehead gently, but with fervent emotion.

As tears filled his eyes he whispered.

"I'm here with you, Maya, an' here I will stay."

He lovingly lifted Eli up into his arms, and while he waited for Maya to awake, he sat beside her and slowly rocked with his son in a chair that he had made.

Noah came into the room and lowered himself onto the raw wood floor, then leaned his broad back against the wall by the glassless but curtained window.

"The doctah says all Maya need be courage an' a desire tah live, an' she be sho tah git well. She gonna mend, Rafe. Ain't a soul in this world bravah 'n Maya. A lil time is all she need. Jus' a lil time."

Brushing away a mosquito from Eli's cheek, Rafe contemplated over this latest calamity.

"Maya has suffahed through so much. She was abused an' violated in slavery, an' endured the cruelties of nature escapin' from that hell. She was chased an' tortured by bounty huntahs, an' now she's been shot by them, but she has always loved her family and friends an' God too. Dear Lord, Noah, we have suffahed near the same. Does God think this be fair? How can this be fair?"

"'Tain't faih, Rafe, life ain't faih. Least ways, not that I evah knowed. Might be, God be leavin' it up tah us tah make things faih, like a tooth foh a tooth an' a eye foh a eye."

The gravity of the dilemma forced a sigh out of Rafe,

"No, no matter what we do, we will nevah be able to make life fair."

Ruth had been standing in the doorway, listening and waiting while she held a bowl of soup for Rafe.

"Seems tah me, the Lawd be doing his best tah make things fair. Everahbody feels pain or sorrow sometime in their lives, but they has joy too. Like that chile in yoh arms, Rafe. We got a good life heah, an' whatevah it took foh us tah get heah, well it wanst easy. Some days were awful bad an' plain terrifying, but I ain't ashamed of it. When Maya wakes, she will tell you, we got a lot tah be grateful foh."

Noah quickly reasoned, "That may be, but I be ready tah take that man's tooth an' eye."

"No, Noah," Ruth mildly reprimanded him, "don't be bringing shame on yohself now. Vengeance ain't gonna make things bettah."

11.

Hurled by a gusting wind, the first raindrops of the late afternoon storm dashed against the Stewart's wagon.

Ben and Sam fought the gusts as they rushed to throw the tarpaulin over the box and secure its corners while Rose and Eyota scrambled to prop up the tar oiled cloth with sticks.

During the worst of the pummeling rain they sheltered beneath the cover, and although the cloth buffeted with the wind and leaked in places, it repelled much of the clamorous torrent.

Fearful and skittish with each roll of thunder and flash of light, the horses walked uneasy in the downpour, their discomfort growing as a finger of the swamp swelled into a knee deep lake under them.

Familiar with the route, the men knew that the trail lay low along the slough for a few more miles, as it had for the past several miles. With many hours of travel yet to go, they took the unavoidable risk that the water wouldn't climb high enough to wash them all away, and they plowed Henry slowly onward to reach Maya in haste for Rose.

By nightfall the rain had ceased, but clouds still shrouded the sky, and the path had disappeared into the water and darkness that surrounded the travelers, convincing them to abandon the effort until daylight.

Ben took grievance with the water as he unhitched Henry and tied his reins to the wagon, but after he and Sam used their blankets to dry the horses, they had no choice other than to leave their animals standing through the night in the newly enlarged swamp.

The two men traded their damp shirts for dry ones, then settled under the tented cloth and into the hay lined bed of the wagon with their wives, but only Sam and Eyota achieved sleep without bother.

Too troubled to be able to ignore the loud choir of chirping frogs and humming cicadas, or the annoying whines and bites from the swarms of mosquitoes, Ben and Rose lay awake in turmoil, heartbroken over their tumultuous reunion with their son and fretful with worry for Maya.

Close beside Ben, Rose wiped the tears from her eyes, and not wishing to awaken Sam or Eyota, she crooned softly.

"I fear that I be a terrible mother. How could I turn our Jonathan away? How could I do such a dreadful thing? What could I have been I thinking? What if we never see him again? What have I done?"

Using a finger to affectionately dab away one of her tears, Ben consoled her.

"We have done what good parents do, Rose. We have called upon him to be answerable for his conduct, in the hope that he shall become a better person."

"But my heart aches so. I feel I shall die."

Despite their friends at the other end of the wagon, and his soggy breeches and the muggy air left by the storm, Ben reached an arm around Rose and drew her close to kiss her cheek tenderly.

"It can be difficult to do the honorable thing even when one knows what that may be, but we are blessed to have the desire for it. Pray for our son, Rose, and for Maya. Pray that they shall be well, and pray that we shall see them both again."

12.

Darian awoke before dawn, but she lay still while she deliberated over what seemed to be her dour, inescapable destiny.

Wrapped in her cloak, in order to defeat the persistent mosquitoes, she bore the heat and listened to what she perceived to be the lonesome calls of birds pleading for a mate as they roused themselves from their solitary night.

Saddened by the birds' tentative cries, and with her hopes for a better life withering, she felt inside her purse for the coin.

It's there. Perhaps this misadventure won't be as disastrous as it seemed to be yesterday.

When the faint glow of morning glimmered above the trees beyond the field, she arose from her sandy bed, tousled her hair, and shook out her cloak.

As she amassed her mane back into the confines of her scarf, she noticed Paolo waiting for her.

In their intent to protect one another, they'd slept near each other on the ground, but the agony of Paolo's wounds had increased with the hardness of his bed, and he'd gone without sleep for much of the night.

He motioned for her to come with him.

"Our walk is far. I've heard that we'll not reach the plantation today."

Darian grimaced in pity at the ugly welts and gashes exposed by the ripped slits of his shirt.

"Are you in pain?"

"No" he lied. "Have your feet healed enough for you to wear shoes?"

She looked down at her shoeless feet.

"Yes" she lied, and her coy smile let him know that she knew he too had lied.

The majority of the marchers were standing, draping all they owned over themselves, and some were asking for food.

John Taggart ladled water from a barrel and doled out pieces of hard biscuit while his helper loaded the wagon, and Hatcher sat on his horse as he ate a wedge of salt pork and slugged down whiskey out of a flask that hung from a chain on his belt. When he drank the last gulp, he cracked his ready whip.

"Get in line! On with the bloody lot of you! To the road you lucky runts! Had the clouds not passed over us in the night, you would all be drowned as rats!"

As he patrolled, he counted heads and bellowed at the people who were slow to obey.

"Get up! Be on with you! 'Twill be a long day, an' longer yet for any idler who begs my whip to cross their back! Jonathan, saddle your horse an' move 'em on!"

Jonathan hesitated before he complied, for he'd acquired a better sense of Hatcher's character, and a clearer understanding of what this new job entailed.

Even though he'd already received a portion of his wage to oversee the march, and given it all to a sentry at the St. Augustine gate, he would have ridden away if not for his attraction to Darian.

He couldn't leave her to be abused by Hatcher or anyone like him.

13.

In the muted light of daybreak, a rooster's proud crow jarred Rafe from his exhausted sleep.

While he'd dozed in the chair beside Maya, Ruth had taken Eli from his lap, but when the floor boards creaked in the morning with the rocking of the chair, Ruth knew that Rafe had awakened and she brought his son back to him.

"Good morning, Rafe."

Accepting Eli, he returned the greeting.

"Good morning Ruth."

"Maya be waking soon, I'm sho of it, an' when she

wakes, she'll be wanting to see you both."

Ruth yawned and rubbed her eyes, and Rafe noticed.

"Have you been up all night?"

"I been checking on her, jus' in case she be needing something."

"I'm grateful to you, an' to Noah, but I want to take her home."

"You be welcome tah stay heah. I can tend tah Eli, an' Noah will fetch anything you need from yoh cabin."

"Thank you, Ruth, but you an' Noah come with us."

Hearing their conversation, Noah poked his head into the room.

"Mo'nin', Rafe. We can carry Maya ovah in a blanket soon as it be light. Be best tah carry her that way. One o' us on each end. Which blanket should I use, Ruth?"

Before Ruth could answer, the cock in the yard announced the day with another boastful crow – and Maya sleepily murmured back to it,

"I'm awake, I'm awake. Enough."

Astonished, Rafe, Ruth, and Noah exclaimed together, as if in one voice,

"Maya!"

Holding Eli tightly, Rafe leaped from his chair and bestowed a gentle, but intensely felt kiss on the young woman he'd loved all of her life.

14.

Awake before the others, Rose quietly looked out from under the tarpaulin, and while the first soft colors of sunrise swept over her, a slight breeze ruffled the few loose curls of her gray streaked brown hair.

As she inhaled the clean air, the tranquil beauty of the rain washed morning brightened her mood and renewed her hope.

She gave Ben's arm a little shake and whispered,

"The horses no longer stand in high water. 'Tis time we be on our way."

Although the flood had receded, the trail had

dissolved into thick sludge, and the wheels of the wagon were sunk well into the muck.

Ben and Sam tried to push the wagon while Henry pulled, but that gained them little progress for the work and almost interred the men in mud.

They wanted to hitch up Amelia next to Henry to ease his burden, but not imagining that both horses would be needed at the same time, they hadn't the rigging to do the job.

After they'd spent an amount of time trying to create a harness for the pair without success, Ben and Sam came to a depressing conclusion, and Rose's outlook plunged as Ben broke the news.

"The mud is too deep for our horses to draw the wagon or even for them to walk in this bog. We cannot trudge through it ourselves in any practical fashion, and in all probability, this mire goes on for leagues. It shall take a day or more to harden enough for us to continue, and longer if there be another storm."

- - - - -

While Rose bided time in the wagon, her despair over the uncertainties of whether Maya still lived or if she would ever see Jonathan again, prompted her to recollect the events of her life; the most pervasive of those being the losses of her children.

As the second evening of their journey neared, and while Ben and Sam were out inspecting the road, she recounted her past to Eyota.

"You be sewn of stouter cord than I, Eyota. This wait is intolerable for me; I worry so for Maya."

"Worry will not change what will be, but I would not counsel you to not worry. You must feel what is in your heart."

"In my heart I know the will of God is for the good, but there be times when 'tis beyond me to understand God's reasons. Years ago, two of our daughters died from measles during an epidemic in Charles Town. Our Charlotte and our Emily were very young and sweet, and I was younger then myself. I thought I would never be happy again, and a long time passed before I could feel joy in my life."

In sad agreement, Eyota commiserated,

"I felt grief much like that when my first husband was attacked and drowned by mercenaries as he fished the Welaka in his canoe."

As Rose imagined that horrible event she shuddered and moaned in empathy, then she went on.

"After I revived from the passing of our young girls, our older daughter, our lovely and shining Hannah, was struck by a carriage and killed. I wondered what sin I had committed to be thrown into such a hell. I lost my desire to live, but Ben's love and that of our sons' saved me and restored my gratefulness. I came to know that our daughters' deaths were not of my making. When our sons grew old enough to go off on their own, I had also grown, in strength and love and in my faith. I shall always miss my children, but I am glad for them and I pray for them, and Jonathan and Maya be a part of those prayers. I hope, someday, my Jonathan shall understand and forgive me for sending him away."

Eyota felt moved by the story and honored that Rose would confide in her. As she and Rose looked into each other's sympathetic eyes, they saw how much they and the sorrows they had experienced were alike even though Eyota had been born a Creek Native and Rose a European, and they spontaneously hugged one another.

Ben and Sam had finished scouting a length of the trail, and at that second, Sam popped his head under the canvas. He chanced to see his wife and Rose in their embrace, and although he knew their feelings were innocent, he couldn't resist the opportunity for a good-natured tease.

"My dear Eyota! Shall Rose and I toss for your affections? I leave for no more than a moment, and you are in each other's arms!"

He tried to act serious, but he couldn't maintain the ruse for long and he burst into laughter.

Eyota playfully jumped at him, but on her way she inadvertently pulled down the tented cloth which they'd left above the wagon to provide shade.

Encumbered by the cloth, she and Sam lost their balance and wound up falling clumsily onto Ben, which helped to break their fall as Ben stood below Sam, and the three of them fell into the slimy mud.

Rose's poignant memories and her deepened friendship with Eyota had brought her almost to tears, but when she looked down from the wagon to see them all laughing and slipping in the mud as they tried to disentangle themselves from the tarpaulin and rise to their feet, she released her pent-up emotions in nearly hysterical laughter.

"You have become giant gingerbread men! If I had a big oven, I would bake you all and take you as presents to Maya!"

The giddy occasion refreshed them, but reminded of the purpose of their mission, Ben rallied some restraint and tried to wipe off his coating of mud.

"With first light we shall be on the road, and God willing, we shall arrive at the village before the sun sets."

- - - - -

In the morning all went well, although, being frugal with their supply of water, neither Sam nor Eyota nor Ben had succeeded in washing all of the muck from themselves. An uncomfortable crust had formed which matted their hair and stiffened their clothes as if they had been starched.

The trail remained muddy, yet not as deep or as sloppy as the previous day.

Their travel was slow, but after a couple of hours the trail wended away from the swamp, and on firmer ground Henry was able to quicken his gait.

With a bright sky to cheer them, and the prospect that she would soon see Maya, Rose began to enjoy the day.

As she and Eyota watched the blue sky soar above and the green grasses pass behind, large white birds glided gracefully overhead and colorful little butterflies flitted about below, but when Ben shouted "Whoa Henry!" that drew the women's attention away from the idyllic exhibition.

"A young pine has fallen and blocks our path," Ben explained, "Sam and I shall have it off the trail shortly."

Sam grabbed the axe that Ben kept strapped to the side of the wagon ever since their run-in with bounty hunters a couple of years before, and he walked over to the fallen tree with Ben.

Ben put his foot on the trunk and gave it a bounce to judge the weight and mobility of it, and Sam took a swing with the axe.

Almost instantly, Ben yelled,

"I am stung! My leg! Dear God, help me! I have never felt such pain from a sting! I've gotten into a nest of hornets and they have stung me all at once!"

Sam's eye caught a movement in the tree, and with a quick swoop of the axe, he neatly chopped off the head of the snake that had bitten Ben.

"Bloody hell, Ben, 'tis a damn viper! We'll have to cut the venom out, and with it a span of your leg."

Rose and Eyota had stood at Ben's alarm, but at Sam's announcement, Rose dropped to her seat in a near faint.

Ben was adamant. "No, no one shall cut off my leg nor any piece of it!"

Eyota took charge. "Lie down Ben. I know what must be done."

After she asked Sam to remove Ben's shoe, his legging, and his stocking, she gave him another errand.

"Ride Amelia to the village, the wagon is slow and it would take too long to clear the path. Go to the medicine man, tell him of the snake and bid him come."

"'Twould be quicker to have Amelia carry us both."

"No, Ben must not move, or the poison might devour him. Hurry, Sam, his life may depend on it."

Before Sam rode off, he gave his word,

"I will do my best, but Amelia is a big girl, and her wide back is built to draft. 'Twill be difficult just to sit her, but I will have the doctor here as soon as can be done."

While they waited for the Native doctor, Rose trembled with worry and her skin became as blanched and damp as Ben's, but as she sat beside him she took his hand, which calmed her as well as comforted him.

Eyota reassured them.

"Good fortune is with us. We are nearer to my village than Saint Augustine. The doctor in the city might have taken Ben's leg, for that is what the white school teaches, but the medicine man of the village will know how to cure him."

When Sam returned with the doctor and the doctor's apprentice, he rode on a faster, borrowed steed, as he'd left Amelia in the village.

Ben had become noticeably ill, and the leg of his breeches had been cut to give room for the swelling. Although he ached in agony with fiery pain, he lay awake and aware of the healer's presence.

Between his moans, he asked the doctor,

"How fares Maya? Does she live?"

"She lives."

Rose let out a quiet, "Thank the Lord," then a quivery, "and my husband?"

As the doctor examined Ben's leg, he also took a look at Ben's stocking and the dead snake that his attendant held up for view.

"One fang marks the skin. This is good. The moccasin did not give all his venom. It might be the mud on the leg cloth hindered the bite."

While herbs burned in a small fire pit, the doctor's apprentice wafted smoke over Ben with a fan of feathers, and as the air became infused with a savory aroma, the medicine filled Ben's lungs.

The doctor carefully rubbed a liquid preparation onto the puncture, then he chose a variety of leaves and more herbs from his bag, chewed them into a mash, and spit the mixture onto the wound.

He brewed a tea of willow bark and herbs, which his assistant held for Ben to drink, then the doctor sang a chant for Ben, in part to soothe him.

To protect Sam from any retributions by the relatives of the deceased snake, the doctor also sang a chant for Sam.

When the doctor finished, he grasped a handful of his horse's mane and jumped up, but before he left with his companion, he advised them.

"What was needed has been done. The sun rides low on its path. Rest him here until the sun returns to mount the sky, then lay him in the wagon and journey on. The worst will come for him this night, but I believe he will live and walk on both legs. In time, we will know."

15.

Although the marchers still wanted to believe the promise of a better life, while they struggled through the three hot and strenuous days on the trail they became disheartened.

Hatcher had threatened to Jonathan that he would disfigure Darian with his whip if he saw them together, and although Jonathan tried to keep watch over her, Darian was saddened by his unexplained distance.

As the afternoon sky grew dreary from yet another storm, the worn-out group arrived at Mosquito Inlet.

They were greeted by the pastoral scene of a

meandering river outlined with hills of white sand, preened land, magnolias, and large, moss garlanded oaks, which astounded them and bolstered their hearts, but for a moment only.

While Hatcher and Jonathan were sent by their superiors to a barracks near the groomed river bank, the marchers were ordered to walk a few miles farther to a much less attractive, wild expanse of thickly overgrown swamp, where they spent the night huddled under trees as they tried to avoid the rain's battering.

At the break of day, the immigrants were immediately forced to labor, and any protests or cries for food resulted in punishment.

The work was grueling, and after a day of toil, with nothing to eat but corn at midday, Darian's threadbare clothes hung on her in shreds and her pocket could be seen through the rents of her skirt.

Worried that someone would take her purse, and with it her coin, she hurried to bury the treasure.

When she felt certain that no one was watching, she pressed the coin into a hole behind a supply hut, and on an impulse, she made a wish.

Bring me love. Bring me a love to share. I will endure this work, this place; I will bear anything, if only I may love and be loved in return.

During the next few days, along with African slaves and other indentured servants, Darian shoveled mud and hacked roots while Paolo felled trees. Amid the scattered groups of laborers, the two friends worked near enough to one another to talk occasionally.

Although Darian felt discouraged by the overwhelming breadth of their chores and by her presumption that Jonathan had forgotten her, Paolo had become despondent as he yearned for Teresa, and he foresaw only more death and despair for the immigrants.

"I have never cowered from work, Darian, but we are no longer on an adventure to build a new world or earn our own land; we've been pirated into a hellish, starving army. We're prisoners, fighting a war against insects and thorns, and tree roots that grip desperate for life, like claws into the earth – and their situation might be less tenuous than our own."

Darian leaned on her shovel and used her torn, dirt stained sleeve to mop the mud and sweat from her cheeks as she agreed.

"I knew we would be servants, but this is not the paradise I thought would be ours when I left my home, or hoped it would be when I endured the misery of our voyage. I saw the beauty of this land as we walked from Saint Augustine, but now I see the horror of living in it."

Paolo took his frustration out on a tree trunk as he swung an axe as forcefully as he was able.

"Will our jailers never feed us more than a bowl of corn or crumb of bread, or ever grant us rest from our labors? Food is plentiful all around us in the woods and sea, but we're not permitted the time to hunt or fish, and if we're discovered foraging, we're beaten. At night, storms soak us and steal our sleep, but that is the best of it, for with the cooling rain we slake our thirsts and bathe ourselves, while our guards drink ale and rum and offer us none but sips of a murky swill they call water."

He took another whack at the tree, which did nothing to allay his anger.

"I don't believe our conditions will improve, but my longing and my fears for Teresa sour my mood. I had imagined her waiting for me by the door of a snug little cottage with food and beer on the table, but that was the simple delusion of a fool. Only dirt, drudgery and the funerals of our brothers and sisters have been waiting for us."

With his next swing, the axe head stuck tight in the tree, and Paolo angrily wrestled it loose then struck the tree again as he continued his complaint.

"We build our houses and ready the land for Doctor Turnbull to farm both at once, and while we labor in hunger in this hot fetid quag, the bugs feed on our blood as a feast!"

An overseer turned to walk toward them and Darian went back to shoveling, but as the man advanced, his interest in Darian became obvious.

Heavily marked with the relics of smallpox, he thrust his scarred face close to hers and flicked his tongue like a lizard.

Repulsed by his actions and the noxious odor that

exuded from his body and his rotted teeth, Darian stood in proud defiance.

Hefting his axe, Paolo warned, "Don't touch her."

But as the overseer drew his pistol from his belt, he laughed.

"Lay down that axe or you'll meet the devil before you speak again."

"Paolo!" Darian begged, "Put it down! Please, put it down!"

Paolo didn't move, but neither did he lay down the axe.

The overseer cocked his gun, and fearing for Paolo's life, Darian blurted out an offer.

"I have something, something of value! I give it to you to not hurt us."

The thought that Darian possessed anything valuable appealed to the man's greed, but her claim seemed dubious.

"What have you that I could want? What have you but rags?"

He kept his pistol aimed at Paolo as he seized Darian by her hair and pulled her sharply with a jerk.

"Speak, wench! What is it you have?"

Taken by surprise, she gasped in pain,

"A coin! A Spanish coin!"

"Show it to me!"

"I hid it," she pointed a distance away to the shed, "there."

He jammed the snout of his pistol into her side and

gave her a shove as he shouted at Paolo,

"Stay as you are! Has she a coin, I'll send her back. Hurl that axe, and its bit will bed in her body while my bullet lodges in yours!"

When Darian produced the coin, the overseer snatched it from her hand, then grabbed a breast and forced his darting tongue into her mouth before he savagely threw her aside.

Feeling violated, yet uninjured and mindful of the consequences of telling or running, Darian walked back to Paolo with her head up, satisfied with her deed.

Paolo called out to her in Greek when she came near.

"Darian! Thank God! Has he harmed you?"

"He took my coin and frightened me, then he slunk away like the vulgar reptile that he is, but I am not hurt."

Paolo hung his head sheepishly.

"I regret that I have brought trouble for you and caused you to lose your coin."

"Feel no blame," Darian reassured him, "the coin is well spent, and I have suffered worse indignities. We are alive and that is all that is important."

Already weakened, Paolo's energy had further waned with the tension of Darian's abduction, and he sank down to sit at her feet.

"Paolo! Are you ill?"

"No, I'm tired and hungry and sore, but all around us our people are starving and dying. There is no help for us here and no hope. Our wasted bodies and even our souls are being consumed by our afflictions. Overseers torture us for their amusement, and Natives raid us in the night to take back their land, the same land promised to us by scoundrels and thieves and a doctor who will not doctor us. Help me find Teresa. Somehow we must all get away from this hell."

16.

Feeling terribly alone on the crowded deck, Teresa
leaned against the wooden railing while small boats
ferried the ship's passengers across the bay of
Mosquito Inlet, and as she waited her turn, she
searched the shore for Paolo and Darian.

The days since her friends disembarked to join the
march had passed excruciatingly slow for her, and the
hot, lonely nights had fomented jealousy toward
Darian and distrust of Paolo.

A battle waged within herself, between her
anticipation of seeing her intended and her new home,

and her worry that Paolo may no longer be in love with her or that Darian might have betrayed her.

Relieved that the frightening journey had finally ended, but fearful of her future, Teresa stepped from the skiff to stand on land for the first time in months, and let fall the tears that she'd bravely held in during the voyage.

I'm here, Mama, I'm in the New World! I wish I could tell you of everything I see and of everything that has happened.

Oh Mama, how I wish you were here with me. My life is dreadfully uncertain, and I am afraid.

If only I could talk with you. If I could hear your voice. If I could awake to the smell of the bread you bake and laugh with you while we sit at the table, or brush your hair for you in the evenings, I would never be a trouble for you Mama, not ever.

Before she could get her bearings, a burly, stubble bearded overseer pushed her forward and snarled,

"Stop yar blubberin'. This be no time far nonsense. Thar's work tah be done an' plenty of it. If ya be wantin' a roof tah sleep under, ya'll work far it! Get in line, over thar. Take yar bags. A mile 'r two tah walk, then ya work! Thar be shovels an' axes far all, an' corn far yar supper."

Unsure of what the man said, other than work, sleep, and supper, Teresa followed the other arriving immigrants.

When she stumbled in the sand, the twig thin yet

energetic young man walking next to her took hold of her arm and steadied her.

"Efharisto" she said quickly, then more deliberately, "Thank you."

"Ah, you are Greek." He spoke in her language as he gave her a better look. "Yes, I see it. I come from Menorca, but I am not like the humble farmers of my country, and the overseers are convinced that I am Greek. I speak Ellinika, but I also speak a little Italiano, and almost as much English as I speak my own Català and Español. My name is Esteban, and I'm sure I have seen you aboard the ship."

They had stopped while they talked, which riled the overseer, and he yelled at them to move on. When he took a few angry strides in their direction, he slid awkwardly in the sand, but with no one to assist him, he fell splay legged onto the beach.

Teresa and Esteban scampered off like mischievous children who had been caught misbehaving, and although Teresa hadn't smiled in days, she prudently stifled a giggle.

"I remember you, Esteban. My name is Teresa. You speak my language well, but I don't speak English well, and the overseers must think me to be stupid."

"Have no concern for what they think, Teresa, they are nothing. If you like, I can teach you the languages I know. I sailed to many ports with my papa, since I was old enough to walk, and my ears listened and learned at every dock. It wasn't long before Papa depended on me to speak for him."

"Is your papa here with you?"

"No, he's grown too old for an adventure, but I'm a boat short of sails without him. This has been the longest and most arduous voyage of my life, and the only one where he hasn't stood beside me. I'm glad he hasn't suffered this journey, but I feel the hole in the air where he should be."

Teresa felt his sadness and matched it with her own.

"I know of that hole. I miss my mama very much, but it was her desire that I come to this land and I couldn't deny her, even though I was afraid."

"Are you afraid now, Teresa?"

"No... yes. I'm not sure how I feel. I have friends who left the ship to march here, but I don't see them and I worry that my heart may be broken."

"Your lover then, and perhaps, a woman friend?"

Impressed by his insight, Teresa nodded while she kept walking, for not far back, the overbearing steward trailed them.

"Paolo and I are betrothed, and I became friends with Darian while we waited for sailing weather in Menorca. I shouldn't worry, for Paolo is an honorable man, but Darian is a beautiful woman, and it is my nature to worry."

"I believe all women worry over love. You say your Paolo is an honorable man? Then I trust that he is not a fool. You are a beautiful woman yourself, Teresa, but it must be your heart that he has fallen in love with, for only a fool loves for beauty alone."

"You flatter me, Esteban, and you are kind, but I pray that you are right, for many men become fools when it comes to love."

Esteban's eyes twinkled with his grin.

"Some women have been known to be similarly affected as well."

17.

Rose had compelled her son to examine his conscience, and after a penetrating look at himself, Jonathan knew that he could neither participate in the brutal mistreatment of the servants and slaves nor be a passive witness to the deplorable conditions in which they were forced to live and work.

He wanted to leave the plantation, but thoughts of Darian had monopolized his mind since he first saw her, and he resolved to take her with him.

She will come with me. I know she will come with me. Her eyes told me everything I need to know.

My God, how she speaks through those eyes, those incredible green eyes!

When I find her, I'll take her from this wretched place and we'll make a life for ourselves somewhere.

Somewhere far from here.

He searched the plantation for Darian, but the enormous property encompassed miles of land where hordes of laborers worked in every direction, on the sandy fields and riverbanks, and in the swamps and forests.

Whenever he looked for her, he knew that Hatcher skulked not far behind, and he had no wish to visit Hatcher's wrath upon her.

When Jonathan finally spotted Darian he refrained from approaching her, but the sight of her toiling in the swamp, wearing the soiled and ragged remnants of her clothing, seared him as if a hot blade had skewered him to his core.

To stay in this madness would surely be death for her. She must come with me; I can't leave her here.

While he waited for the opportune moment, he pretended to be attentive to his duties, but he spent hours gambling in the barracks where day or night a man could join in the games played by the overseers.

The dice favored Jonathan, and when his pouch fattened with the wagers the men had lost (and Hatcher was elsewhere), he deemed it to be the right time to declare himself to Darian and make their escape.

He began to leave the room, but a pock scarred overseer, enraged over his losses, bared his knife and his notched teeth.

"Stand fast! Another game to redeem my silver, or prepare to forfeit your purse in a manner which will not amuse you."

Anxious to reach Darian while Hatcher couldn't interfere, and with the hope that the man would relent from his position, Jonathan smiled and made light of the threat.

"I did not cheat you, Marcus. Anyone here will vouch that I play an honest game, but if we throw the dice now you are sure to lose for luck is with me. I will gladly compete with you tomorrow, even though tomorrow good luck may desert me."

Marcus's grimace appeared fiercer as he stabbed at the air with his blade, and while he moved closer to Jonathan, a few of the other men took steps away.

Jonathan tried another tack.

"Allow me my luck today, for a pretty lass awaits my company and I've kept her waiting too long."

"A wench is it? One of those bloody servant whores? Are you a half-wit or a simpleton? Some of those harlots are fair to the eye, but to make an arrangement with one? You must be daft! Throw one down when the urge comes to you then leave her in the dirt where she belongs!"

Some of the men laughed, but Jonathan felt a compulsion to run Marcus through, and a string of insults came to his mind, but his desire to rescue Darian prevailed over his inclination.

"You may think me a fool, but I prefer the maid be willing. Permit me my folly today, and let us resume our games tomorrow."

Marcus grudgingly yielded his stance and lowered his knife.

"Go on with you. Have your trollop. I'll see to it that I gain back your winnings soon enough."

18.

Sickened by the snake's poison, Ben moaned in his intermittent slumber, which seemed to be more stupor than sleep, but neither the Stewarts nor the Coxes slept much during the agonizing night in the forest.

When the sun climbed high enough to light the narrow trail between the trees, they traveled onward, and in an effort to not jostle Ben more than necessary, Sam drove the wagon as slowly as the night had seemed to pass.

Despite her weariness, Rose found solace in her belief that inasmuch as Ben had survived the night, he would live through this trial, and her anxiety transformed into a stoic acceptance of Ben's condition and a resigned forbearance toward their delay in reaching Maya.

When the wagon came into view from the cabin, Rafe went out to greet them, but his glad reception turned sober as soon as he saw that Ben was injured.

In a short procession, Rafe and Sam carried Ben inside while Rose and Eyota led the way, and after the two women made a mattress on the floor for Ben out of a folded blanket, Rafe told them about Maya's ordeal and how she bravely endured even though the bullet remained in her back.

Ben asked to see her, but he fell asleep directly after he asked, and Rose went alone into the other room, where Maya's small body made her little bed seem large.

"Miz Rose, you came!"

"How do you feel, my child?"

"Bettah with you here, Miz Rose."

Rose smiled, but her manner became solemn.

So lovely, and so fragile. I would take her into my arms, but I fear I might hurt her.

As she bent over Maya, she carefully took the young woman's hand and held it lightly against her cheek for a moment.

"I am told that bounty hunters shot you."

Maya shook her head yes, then no.

"They nevah knew I was there. I was hidin' in the

brush when one of 'em shot at a deer. He missed, an' the bullet come to me."

"Did you see the man?"

"I could only hear 'em talkin', but the man who shot the gun was named Hatchah."

Somewhat relieved to hear that it hadn't been Jonathan who shot Maya, Rose sat down on the chair beside Maya's bed, and Maya changed the subject as she nodded toward a large basket.

"See how Eli has grown. Noah brought a biggah basket from the village foh him."

"You have a handsome son, Maya, as handsome as his father."

"I want him tah be strong like Rafe too."

"He shall be. See how he holds his head at such an early age? He has the strength of a calf."

Rose lifted him up, kissed him and cooed at him, then laughed,

"Soon he shall weigh as much as one!"

Had it been dark, Maya's pride would have illuminated the room.

"Where is Mistah Ben? I want tah see him an' show him Eli."

"He sleeps in the other room. We met with some misfortune on the trail and Ben faced the worst of it, but you are well acquainted with the dangers of the woods for your experience in the wilderness far exceeds our own. A snake has bitten my Ben, but the doctor has ministered to him and there be no need for worry."

"A snake! Not worry? Mistah Ben be like a fathah tah me, an' the only fathah I have known. Please, Miz Rose, I must go tah him."

"I understand your need, Maya, but Ben must have his sleep, and he shall be well shortly, as shall you be if you keep to your bed. Eyota wisely says that advice should not keep us from listening to our hearts, but you must be patient. Rest while I do my chores. I would stay with you now, but our clothing and blankets carry the mud of the road and need be washed while the sun may dry them. Mud! Dear Lord, such mud! The wagon got stuck in a bog, and while it sat, Sam and Eyota toppled down from the box by accident and landed on Ben. How you would have laughed with me to see them wallowing in the mud. The more they tried to help each other out of the slop the more they dug themselves into it, but when the wash is done, I shall tell you the stories of everything we have seen and done since last we came."

Rose placed Eli back in the basket and gave Maya's hand a gentle squeeze, then left the room before Maya could see her emerging tears.

- - - - -

Ben took only a brief nap, but when he looked up from his bed, he needed a moment to remember where he was and how he'd come to be there.

His pain had subsided a bit, but checking his leg, he

saw that the swelling hadn't lessened.

*My poor misshapen leg, an ugly bruise over much of it,
and my favorite pair of breeches cut. Ah, better the
breeches than my leg.*

He tried to bend his knee, and when it moved he was
reasonably surprised.

He called for Rose, but Rose was outside, draping the
washed clothing and blankets over some bushes and
ropes to dry, and no one answered him.

Noah and Ruth had come over from their cabin, but
while Ruth and Eyota were scrubbing the wagon and
the muddy tarpaulin, Noah had taken Henry to the
river to bathe him, and Sam had walked to the village
to get Amelia.

Ben made a futile attempt to rise then he called for
Rose again, but stiff and slow, it was Maya who came.

"Mistah Ben! I'm awful glad yoh here. Is there
somethin' I can do foh you? Ooh, Mistah Ben, yoh leg!
That looks awesome painful. I'm sorry you been bit, an'
I'm sorry it happened on yoh way tah see me."

"Thank you Maya, but my leg shall heal and my heart
is well, for I'm glad to be here. Are you well?"

She coughed a little, but said,

"I feel much bettah now that you an' Miz Rose are
here."

Her optimism aside, her cough bothered Ben, and his
smile became a gentle frown as her careful movements
confirmed her pain.

"Rose would disapprove of you being about. You

should get back to your bed."

"You are right, Mistah Ben, Miz Rose will fuss even though I been in bed foh days, but I want you to see Eli. He's biggah than any melon in the garden!"

The thought retrieved Ben's smile.

"When everyone comes inside, I shall ask Rose to bring him to me, and if she allows it, we shall have Rafe carry you here. Go to bed now, before Rose sees you. She can be as strict as a prison guard," he teased, "and I will not have her scolding at us!"

19.

Laboring in the mire and heat of a swamp rife with insects brought agony for Teresa, and being too afraid of the overseers and wild animals to wander in search of Paolo or Darian, her meager and lonely existence wrought a closer bond between her and Esteban.

The days seemed too long and the nights too short, but only in the shadows of an evening's campfire would Teresa dare to exchange more than a few words with him.

"This place is beyond any abomination I could imagine, but I'm thankful to have you with me. I'm not strong enough to bear this alone."

"You are strong, Teresa, tell yourself you are strong. We are strong, and we are brave. We made it across the sea in that reeking, crowded ship, and we made it to this shore. Each blistering day brings us closer to having our own land, our own farms, and our own lives. Soon we'll be living in the houses we build and everything will be better. We can make it through this."

"Nothing in my life has ever been so hard. All that is left of me are aching bones and a fragile heart that feels heavier than the shovelfuls of dirt I lift. I need food and sleep, and I long for my home and my mother and Paolo.

"Paolo is here somewhere. He must be searching for you. I will ask everyone I meet if they know of him. He will find you."

"You see how I rely on you, Esteban? What would I do without you, my young brother?"

For a moment, Esteban felt the heaviness of his own heart, as he'd developed feelings for her which were not brotherly, and Teresa heard the wounded pride in his voice when he next spoke.

"I am not so young. I'm a man of 16 years. Old enough to sail the sea, cut down trees and build houses, and to marry, if I choose."

"You are very much a man, and a fine one as well. Forgive me if I have offended you. I meant only that you are younger than I and so great a friend that I regard you dearly as my brother."

Esteban didn't disclose his innermost thoughts.

A brother. She thinks of me as a brother! I boast of my strength and bravery, but I haven't the courage to confess that I hope she'll feel differently about Paolo when she sees him again, and I would marry her myself.

Rising above his bruised feelings, he gave her his best, brotherly support.

"All is well between us. Sleep now, and tomorrow Paolo will find you."

20.

Angus McGinn hadn't come home for his supper or his afternoon nap, and while his plate laid cold on the table, a taper dwindled down to a small stub of wax.

Alone in the candle's waning light, Letticia McGinn sat hugging a bottle of cane spirits to her chest. Her breath reeked of the rum, and her mind fumed with anger.

As she pictured her absent husband frolicking in a tavern, trifling with some other woman, she wailed to the vacant air.

"You'll regret this, Angus, you poor excuse for a

husband. Derelict you are, derelict! If not for me, you'd have no money for the beer you drink. You spend your days in the taverns, but when your stomach growls with hunger, you stagger home and expect me to feed you before you stumble to bed. I treat you like a king, while you humiliate me in town! Never again, Angus McGinn. Never again!"

A few more swigs emboldened her, and while the delusions of her drink gave her no doubt that she could rout any ruffian she might meet along the way, she set a fresh candle into a lantern and careened up the road in search of Angus.

Even though Lettie managed to navigate the mile to the nearest tavern without incident, she remained unsteady on her feet, and when she pushed against the heavy entry door of the public house, she propelled into the building.

Tumbling stern over bow, she let out a screech just before her head hit hard on the floor, and with her skirts luffing like loose sails in the wind, she foundered into a heap.

A moment of shock silenced the four inebriated patrons inside – then the small group erupted with raucous laughter.

When the odd pile didn't move, a rugged looking rogue standing near her lifted the layer of skirt that covered her head.

"'Tisn't a pretty wench, and round as a tub, but a wench it be."

Seeing Lettie's face, the man's female companion smiled in amused condescension.

"I know her, Scully. She's the wife of Angus McGinn. Poor Angus, he can find no escape from her, though like most of this town, he tries. To be sure, she's here looking for him. How timely of Angus to be elsewhere."

One of the more intoxicated men proposed, in jest,

"We could do Angus a great favor if we removed her from Saint Augustine."

A cheer of accord arose from his miscreant friends, and the barkeeper retreated into the storeroom to maintain his customary neutral position.

The third man offered a scheme.

"I can smell the rum in 'er from 'ere. 'Twill be noon afore she awakes. An 'ogshead what fell an' broke stands in my wagon, an' 'twould fit 'er fine, just a bit of work to strap it up an' 'oist 'er in. 'Twould be no large a loss to me. The bloody cooper wants an arm to fix an' patch the thing, yet it may ne'er serve for spirits again patch or no, an' I'll na' pay his price. But if we buy a bottle of rum for the guard, we'll 'ave no trouble at the gate when we ride the sot through."

As they snickered at the joke and the cleverness of themselves, they bandied about where to take her.

Then Scully put forward what seemed to be the easiest option.

"I had drinks with a mate whose ship be takin' supplies to Mosquito Inlet, and they're sailin' soon with the tide at sunrise. Stuff her in the barrel and haul

111

her to the hold. I'd rather a mate drink the rum than a guard. We'll miss the gate and a long ride altogether, and Angus will be rid of her for days!"

In an uproar of drunken laughter they unanimously approved the plan and gave no thought to what their design might bring for Lettie.

All the while, Lettie lay furled in her skirts, aground on the floor, and completely unaware of her forthcoming deportation.

21.

A rumor spread among the indentured servants of Dr. Turnbull that the next supply ship to arrive in Mosquito Inlet would be commandeered by Italian mutineers of the settlement and its sails would be set for Cuba, where food and medicine were plentiful, and the wish to homestead their own land could come true for anyone who would enlist with them.

A similar story had brought the immigrants to the inlet from Europe, but after existing in more sordid conditions at the doctor's plantation than those they'd left behind, a number of settlers accepted the tale out of desperation, and they were eager to aid in the rebellion.

The alluring proposition had easily persuaded Paolo. He'd longed for an escape since his first day at the plantation, and his illness had progressed to where he could no longer deny his debility to himself or to Darian.

"Rally with us, Darian, we must take this chance. The talons of death clutch at my shoulder like a vulture impatient for the catch, and I fear tragedy awaits for everyone enslaved here. My only hope to live on is to mutiny with the others and seek treatment in Cuba. I don't want to sail without Teresa, but I can't be her husband if I am ruined by disease. If I cannot find her, I must board the ship without her."

Sweating profusely from his fever, a chill shook him violently, and Darian witnessed the grim truth of his infirmity, but she artfully hid her anguish for him in gentleness.

"Don't talk to me of mutiny, or of leaving Teresa. She loves you and you need her, don't forsake her. To plunder a ship would bring a greater risk of death than your illness. Do not be a part of it. I will ask for Doctor Turnbull to attend you. He will cure you, and I will find Teresa for you."

As she gave Paolo a hug for encouragement, Jonathan came riding near, ready to run away with her if she would go with him, but while he watched them embrace he misinterpreted their emotion.

114

Stopping his horse, he sat immobile, unable to turn away.

I have lost her.

No, I'm a fool, she was never mine to lose.

I should have tried harder to loose myself from Hatcher sooner, and perhaps I enjoyed the dice too much.

I filled my pouch with coins for a future together, but what good is silver if I have squandered our future?

When I looked into her eyes, all the world disappeared except for her, and time itself stood still. Never have I felt so strange before, nor so glorious. Her eyes told me her heart. Why didn't I tell her mine?

My God, I'm worse than a fool! My foolishness might have cost Darian her life!

Whether to ride away or go to her, his uncertainty became resolved in a moment of perception.

I can't leave knowing that I'll never see her again. I can't live thinking that I left her here to die. I would fight an army to spare her. One man will not stop me.

Risking rejection, he asked his mount to walk forward.

As his horse neared Darian she recognized it, and when she realized that the man sitting upon the steed was Jonathan, her heart began to beat faster.

She took a few steps in his direction and away from Paolo, and greeted him with a hopeful, slender smile.

"You have not forgot me, Jonathan."

He got down from his saddle and stood close to her,

115

facing her, almost touching her, and felt as if he had been pulled to her.

"I would never want to forget you."

"Can you help Paolo? He needs medicine and my friend Teresa we cannot find. They are in love."

With her request, Jonathan's spirit soared, and as he looked down into her expressive eyes once more, he knew, they too were in love.

"I will bring them both to you."

22.

Letticia awoke inside the belly of the hogshead barrel and in the bowels of a ship's hold. The total darkness and the constraints of her position added to her half-awake, and still a bit tipsy, confusion.

Deep below decks and caged in the barrel, she heard nothing but a drone in her ears.

What manner of prison is this? Where am I? Be I blind and bound, or in hell? If this be a coffin, 'tis surely not made for me.

Queasy and cramped, with her body folded and her quantity of skirts bunched into every cranny, she did her best to push against the sides of the barrel as she hollered for help.

Her shouts increased the throbbing pain in her head and brought no one, but she managed to rock the barrel over, which loosed the poorly repaired staves and the rope that had been tied around them.

Pieces of the barrel fell away, but the blackness persisted as she groped to free herself from the parts that remained.

Her senses clearer, she caught the dank odor of mildew and the sound of water as it splashed inside the hull, and she felt the pitch of the ship as it sailed.

A ship. How have I come to be on a ship?

She floundered about the hold, sightless in the dark, while she rapped with one of the broken staves. When the only response was the groan of a timber, she sat down on a crate, bruised and miserable.

Am I to spend eternity on a ghost ship in hell? Dear Lord, why are you punishing me? I have done nothing wrong. Nothing!

Oh, I see the means of it. This be Angus's doing! My useless husband has had me kidnapped!

She pounded with the stave, and as she shook a demanding finger at the black void, she screamed,

"You wait till I am home, Angus McGinn! You shall never regret anything in your life as much as you will regret this! I shall have you thrown into a pit as dark as this one, and there you will rot!"

A blast of light flooded in from overhead and Lettie

shielded her eyes as a gruff voice thundered from the opened hatch.

"Bloody hell, a woman!"

A rope ladder dropped down and the voice yelled, "Take hold and climb up."

But Lettie wouldn't embark on the lofty and frightful climb.

The voice roared, "Climb up! Beggars who stow aboard ship will work for their passage."

Lettie retorted with impudence.

"'Twas no intention of mine, sir, to sail on your stinking ship! I am kidnapped and I cannot climb!"

The voice gave an angry reply.

"An unlikely story. Stay there and starve then, and the captain will sell you off in the end!"

The hatch cover slid back into place and shut with a thud, and an obstinate Lettie sat in the lightless hold, quietly plotting her revenge on Angus – until she heard the scuffling and squealing of rats.

Already angered, her fear spawned a rampage. She shrieked and thrashed to keep the rats away as she tore at baskets, tipped crates over, and threw any cargo that she could lift.

In the midst of her furor, the hatch opened again and a considerably disgruntled sailor descended on a net that hung from a boom.

Scowling at the destruction, he motioned toward the net with his pistol as he spoke tersely through tight teeth.

"Get in. The captain requires your presence on deck."

- - - - -

Hoisted out of the hold and suspended a few feet above the deck, Lettie clung to the inside of the net as she endured a round of jeers from the crew, but the men were quick to silence themselves when the captain strode out from his cabin.

Before he could say a word, Lettie took advantage of the lull and went on a tirade.

"Release me! I demand release! Return me to Saint Augustine at once! 'Tis through treachery that I be aboard your ship. I am kidnapped! I am a married woman of good standing in the city and a friend of the constable. Release me, or be charged with the crime!"

The captain was unmoved.

"Madam, your threats are pointless. I am the law on this ship. I can force you to work for your passage or throw you back down the hold in chains! Or, I could sell you off to the highest bidder, if a man would find you worthy of the buy."

He raised his hand for attention and addressed the crew.

"What say you men? Who bids for this willful harpy?"

A few men howled, while others hooted taunts, then the captain waved his hand for quiet, and his sarcastic smile distorted into a more ominous smirk as he suggested another course to Lettie.

"Perhaps you would rather swim to shore, or be

swallowed up by sharks?"

Lettie responded with rage.

"I am wronged! You must return me to Saint Augustine! Return me now!"

Irritated by her commands, the captain ended the conflict with indifference.

"You have no say in this matter; the judgement is mine. You'll scrub the heads and swab the decks, and be put ashore at Mosquito Inlet."

23.

A ray of sunrise split the sky as rioting mutineers cleaved their way into a storehouse of the plantation at Mosquito Inlet.

Frantically, they grabbed the hoarded food and casks of rum inside, and loaded the guns that were stocked there with the ammunition they found piled beside.

In a frenzy, they ate and drank what they could, and while they ran crazed with their booty to the river, they hurled food and casks and guns to other laborers.

Shots were fired by mutineers and overseers alike.

Too ill to join in the mutiny, Paolo cheered when he

heard the distant fray, but since his tender reunion with Teresa and his receipt of the medicine that Jonathan had procured from the stores of the barracks, he was willing to remain at the plantation.

Swarming into the several small boats that were tied up along the river's edge, the mob of unruly insurgents headed their rebellious armada toward a sloop moored offshore and a schooner that had anchored in the harbor at sunset the night before.

Volleys of bullets flew back and forth across the bay, but the weight of the raided schooner's new passengers added to that of the unloaded cargo and caused the ship to draw too deep a draft to cross the submerged mound of sand at the mouth of the inlet.

Much of the goods were thrown overboard in a feverish attempt to pass over the bar and reach the open sea.

When a cannon was fired at the trapped schooner, marauders staved the casks of rum they had saved for themselves and clambered into a large canoe.

Others jumped overboard, swam for shore, and ran.

While frightened screams and the angry yells of rioters filled the harbor, smoke and the acrid stench of burning sulfur and gun powder choked the air.

In the chaos, Jonathan rode to Darian, and with great daring, swept her up onto his horse and fled with her into the woods.

24.

The tremendous force of a cannon ball as it pierced the schooner's hull, jolted Letticia out of the tiny compartment she'd hidden in when the mutineers at Mosquito Inlet surged onto the ship.

In the mayhem of the battle and the havoc of the ship's demolition, Lettie braced herself to jump overboard, but her fear of the water surpassed her fear of being shot, and she stood in a daze at a splintered section of the rail while she watched others make the leap.

When fire began to eat at the deck, one of the fleeing

J.S. Lavallee

rebels grabbed her and took her with him as he vaulted over the side.

Underwater and disoriented, Lettie panicked as her tiers of clothing twisted with the current and pulled her downward. By instinct, she reached out and swirled her arms, and by luck, her rescuer grasped one of them.

When he brought her to the surface she gasped for air, and sputtered while he towed her to a spit of sand on the south side of the inlet.

"Get up!" He yelled in Catalan, "Run! Run for your life!"

Lettie didn't understand his warning, but she got up to get out of the water and stood dripping on the sand.

"I am British," she told him, in her usual haughty style, "and I live in Saint Augustine."

The gaunt young man spoke again, this time in English.

"Run for your life! The overseers will not care who you are or where you live. You will be killed or made a slave!"

As he set off running down the beach, a bullet sped past Lettie. Startled by the near miss, she screamed after him,

"Help me! I cannot run!"

"Walk then!" He shouted back, "I saved your life, now I save my own!

Hoping to hide between the hills of sand which divided the sea from the harbor, Lettie shuffled to the nearest break in the ridge, and just as she dropped into a cover of tall grass between the dunes, her rescuer arrived there to accompany her.

Unaccustomed to acknowledging her appreciation, she blundered through an introduction.

"I am Letticia McGinn, and my husband will not thank you for saving me."

"My name is Esteban," he said with a chuckle, "and I will not tell him."

Wasting no time, Esteban climbed a knoll to scout for a route of escape, and as he knelt in the sand, he cautiously peered over the top.

Fugitives speckled the beach like ants as they ran, and a sloop filled with jubilant mutineers sailed by on its way to Cuba, but at the bay's shore near where he and Letticia hid, six armed overseers landed in three skiffs and began to spread out over the slim peninsula.

At the likelihood of his and Lettie's imminent capture, Esteban whispered to himself,

"We may not thank me either, Letticia."

But when the overseers passed by them without noticing them, and the skiffs sat on an otherwise empty beach, the opportunity for escape seemed providential.

Esteban tugged Lettie across the sand with as much haste as he could coax from her, but when he skidded a boat into the bay, the overseer who had stayed to guard the skiffs, jumped up from the one in which he'd been reclining.

Holding Esteban and Letticia at gunpoint, and with the objective of recovering the errant unmanned boat, the overseer sat on the more forward of the center seats as he forced Esteban to shove the skiff into the bay.

Amid Letticia's protests that she was a British citizen, not an indentured Menorcan, and while still held in the overseer's line of fire, Esteban then struggled in waist deep water to heave his self-imposed charge up and into the boat.

The little craft lurched sharply, but as the overseer tried to regain the boat's balance and his own, his gun no longer pointed at Letticia or at Esteban, which gave Esteban the idea to cause the skiff to capsize.

He hefted himself up with a vigorous leap, and his action overturned the boat with a powerful launch. The rim of the skiff clouted the overseer on his head, which rendered him senseless, but Esteban's lunge also drove the boat away from shore and tossed Lettie into deeper water.

Esteban chose to help Lettie, but after he pulled her to shallow water, his conscience sent him back to the boat to rescue the overseer.

He found only an oar floating in the bay, and not the overseer, but he discovered a space of trapped air beneath the skiff.

Scanning the beach, he didn't see that overseer or any others, and he prodded the boat closer to shore as he called out to Letticia,

"Come, hold onto the boat!"

"I will not," she whined, "I'll not get into that water nor shall I get in that stupid boat."

"This is our chance, Letticia, hurry! We can hide under it and get away. There is air. You can hold onto a seat and your head will be above the water."

Aghast at the thought, Lettie declined, and Esteban left the skiff behind as he waded to shore.

"I won't leave you. We'll walk together to the woods."

Lettie studied the sad submission in his sunken cheeks and surveyed the wet bits of clothing pasted to his overly thin young body, and after she scrutinized her own hardened heart, she performed what may well have been the first unselfish act of her adult life.

"Swim to the boat, Esteban. You saved my life, now go and save your own. I am British, I shall be safe, but you... no, you must go. I will tell Doctor Turnbull that I am a woman of prominence in Saint Augustine, and he shall provide me with an escort to the city."

Esteban conceded to the futility of his argument, and as the boat began to wander farther from the beach, he bowed to the benevolent turn in her behavior.

When he reached the skiff he waved, and just loud enough for her to hear, he yelled,

"Good luck be with you, Letticia."

Then he impelled the boat along while he swam under it, and the little skiff appeared to be an abandoned wreck as it seemed to drift down the bay upside down.

He never saw the two overseers who came upon Lettie as she stood on the beach watching him float away, but while the two overseers and their four captives trudged across the sand, Lettie waited for them at the bay's edge.

When they arrived, she took up an unassuming pose, which for her, was a challenge.

"Help me, sirs. I am a British citizen. I have been kidnapped, and I wish to be returned to my home and husband in Saint Augustine."

The two overseers looked at each other with surprise, then broke into laughter. One of them pointed to the remaining beached boat while the other gave her a shove.

"Get to that boat, woman! Don't waste our time with babble."

Despite the offense, Lettie kept her composure, but she gave up her facade of humility.

"I am not an indentured servant. Hear me, look at me. 'Tis a well fed British woman I am, and over there in the harbor burns the ship that held me against my will."

She pointed to the ship, but the fire had been extinguished.

With sand clumped onto the hems of her drooping skirts, her sodden hair clinging wildly to the sides of her face, and her hands raw with sores from scrubbing the decks and heads of the ship, her bedraggled and drenched appearance seemed to be very much that of a renegade servant of the plantation.

One of the overseers gestured with his gun to urge her again to walk.

"I say your home is here and you be a mutineer like the rest of these bloody beggars."

"I am British, I swear it. I ask for an audience with Doctor Turnbull that he should send me home."

"An audience with the doctor?" he scoffed. "You fancy yourself to be royalty!"

The other overseer chimed in with mockery,

"Meet her highness the queen, ruler of tatters and rags. You'll work wench, or you'll starve as you sit in a squalid jail!"

Lettie's cheeks flushed, and she came close to losing her temper, but she paled with a shock that shivered her to the bottom of her empty stomach as she began to comprehend the seriousness of her circumstance.

I be a stubborn fool! Why didn't I listen to Esteban? Perhaps, were I to offer a reward...

"My dear and loving husband will gladly pay a reward to the gentleman who brings me home."

The overseers paused their steps, and Lettie quickly enhanced the pot.

"Yes, a generous reward, and a meal right and proper for a king! My skill in the kitchen is known throughout the city and beyond. It may be that the food here is adequate, even tolerable, but the meals I prepare be an unforgettable delight. I shall select from the butcher his tender most meats and from my garden my best herbs and vegetables for your delicious feast, and you shall have sweet cakes and a bottle of the finest cane spirits. Now, which of you gentlemen shall escort me home and claim the reward?"

"Not I" they replied simultaneously, and as they walked behind Lettie and the quartet of previously captured runaways, each overseer spoke under their breath to the other.

"That wench can spin a tale."

"Aye. That she can, that she can."

"Do you think any of it be truth?"

"Nah. Not a whit, not a whit."

25.

Darian leaned into Jonathan and held on tight while they raced through the woods on his horse, and although they didn't speak, they felt no need for it.

They hadn't had time for courtship, but neither had they any reason for wiles, nor a wish by either of them to deny the truth of their love or the magnitude of their actions.

Never before had Darian felt so exhilarated or so in love, and she treasured every moment.

This is what I have wished for, prayed for, to be loved and love in return. To feel his body against mine and know my heart beats with his is worth every risk I have ever taken and every hardship I have ever endured.

While their flight absorbed them, the excitement of new love enthralled them, and even though their fears of being apprehended by overseers or hostile Natives weren't erased, the hazards in the forests and swamps seemed minor in comparison to the perils of life at the plantation.

Avoiding the road whenever they could, but not straying far from it, Jonathan became engrossed in finding their way safely through the intricate maze of water, scrub palms and trees. He clenched his jaw in determination and pressed his horse onward as they strove to get away.

When the sun reached its summit, they rested a short time and fortified themselves with a little food and drink, and while Darian watched Jonathan care for his horse and praise him for carrying them through such grisly terrain, she grew even more in love.

When night began to veil their path, they took refuge in the woods, and Jonathan draped his blanket around Darian, given that little was left of her clothes.

She wanted to share the blanket with him, but he insisted that she keep it for herself, and the gesture earned him her complete devotion.

While they nestled together in the darkness, a slice of moon peeked between the tree tops, and Jonathan spoke softly about his thoughts and his plans for their future.

"Hunters will be looking for runaways, and some of the men will be searching on horseback. I don't believe any of them would have come as far as we have this day, but I would not gamble on it. Should anyone come near, could you pretend to be my prisoner?"

Understanding only part of what he said, Darian gave him a sweet, but bewildered smile as she replied mostly with her eyes.

"If you say I am your prisoner, I am your prisoner."

As he looked into her trusting eyes, Jonathan knew that in truth, his heart had become her captive.

The emotional moment moved him and he lovingly lifted her chin.

"When I look into your eyes, I see the most beautiful eyes I have ever seen, and I feel the goodness of your soul so deeply that I weep to know what you have suffered. I want to keep you from harm and make a good home for you, and I pray that our children shall have your eyes. All will be well for us. I promise you this with all of my heart."

That Darian knew little of Jonathan's language and Jonathan understood less of hers was of no importance. In the blissful rapture of their first kiss, their fears added fervor to their passion, and their worries temporarily melted away.

26.

Caught by overseers, a ragged group of escapees were corralled, and as they were being herded back to the plantation in defeat, Teresa saw Esteban walking among them.

Despair and fear pealed in her voice as she yelled, "Esteban, Esteban!"

When their eyes met, Esteban could see that she was crying.

As he tried to make his way past the other captives to get to her, an overseer placed himself in his path.

Teresa tried to reach out to Esteban, but the

overseer used the stock of his rifle to block her, and she screamed in Greek,

"They must not take you Esteban! Don't let them hurt you!

Crumpling to her knees, she sobbed to him,

"Paolo has died. He died in my arms in the night, and Darian ran away in the mutiny. Dear God, Esteban, I will die here without you!"

In English, Esteban implored of the guard,

"Her husband died last night. She has no one but me. Let me speak with her a moment."

The overseer sneered in disapproval, but he thought that Esteban would likely be hanged, and although Teresa's eyes were swollen and red from weeping, her beauty was evident.

With a show of arms, he gave in to Esteban's request with a caution,

"A moment, no more."

Esteban helped Teresa to rise, and as she clung to him with desperation, he whispered in her ear.

"I am dearly sorry that you have lost Paolo. I know how much you have loved him. Remember his love, and let his love give you strength. Paolo would want you to live. Can you be brave for him?"

"I will try."

But in her heart, she pled to her mother.

Oh Mama, how do I live without Paolo? How do I live without his love, his voice... and the touch of his skin? How can I live in this horrible place without him?

Oh Mama, how did you live without Papa? How did you live without his love?

When the overseer pulled Esteban away, Teresa couldn't stem the flow of her tears. She fell to her knees again and prayed.

Save him, Lord, please save him.

Esteban saw her fall, and his heart broke for her. As he drew on his own courage, he shouted back to her,

"They will release me, I promise you. I'm worth more to them alive. I will stay with you and I will build a house for you. Wait for me, Teresa, I love you."

The truth and depth of his declaration struck her.

Mama, is this your guidance?

This ache I feel for Paolo is greater than any torture I have suffered, but Esteban is so very kind, I do love him. Not as he loves me, and not with the same love I feel for Paolo, but if I am to survive I will need Esteban's help more than ever, and I think he needs me.

In time, I could learn to love him differently than as a brother.

While she considered the future, she assumed some of Esteban's fearlessness, and bravely, she stood to call to him.

"Esteban! I will be here! I will be here waiting for you!"

27.

Her fair skin burned red by the sun and bloodied from the cuts and scratches of thorns and sharp fronds, Letticia labored in disbelief at her state of affairs.

After her capture she'd been sent straight to the fields, and while she shoveled in half-hearted attempts to uproot thickets, she begged any overseer who came near her to return her to St. Augustine or take her to Dr. Turnbull.

She was ridiculed or ignored, and repeatedly threatened, but she convinced no one.

When a rough and weathered overseer astride a

horse heard her pleas, he rode up to her.

"There! Woman! What is this bloody clatter you make? Do you ask for my whip to quiet you?"

"Sir, I am kidnapped. That I be here is a horrible mistake. All I want is to go home to Saint Augustine. My husband will pay you well for your trouble, and I shall reward you with the finest supper you shall ever eat."

The overseer arched a brow.

"An' what be the name of your husband?"

"Angus McGinn is my husband, and I am Letticia McGinn."

His brash laughter unnerved her, and she cringed as she prepared for a lashing, but he held back the switch.

"Ha! I suspected such. Call me Hatcher. I've met your husband, Missus McGinn. He spoke of you an' your admirable cookery when we drank together at a public house in Saint Augustine."

"Dear Lord! Dear Mister Hatcher! Rescue me, sir, save me, take me to my home." Then Lettie said a word she rarely used, "Please."

As he considered Lettie's plea and her plump size, his horse frisked with impatience, and Hatcher himself seemed ready to resume their ride.

"Undoubtedly, Angus grieves for your fine meals, but my horse cannot carry the two of us, an' you could not walk the distance in a week. To arrange a means of conveyance would take some contrivin'."

To keep Hatcher from leaving, Lettie bargained,

"Do not desert me, sir! I, I will feed your horse as well as you, and you shall have sweet cakes with your supper and a bottle of the best cane spirits in the city!"

The uprising had devastated the rations of rum for the overseers of the plantation, and Hatcher's personal reserve was down to less than a flask. He'd already thought of riding to St. Augustine to replenish his supply under the pretext of searching for mutineers, but he believed that he would find Jonathan there with Darian, and his interest in them had become consuming.

He countered her offer.

"A fair purse, two meals with rum, an' two bottles to spare."

As if the wind had filled her sails, Lettie took a breath, and inhaled hope.

"You shall have it, Mister Hatcher."

Then she promptly exhaled apprehension.

'Tis a grand order I must fill. Money, meals, and three bottles of rum. Perhaps more. What if Angus has found the coins and spirits I hide? If every penny is spent and every drop of rum drunk, I'll not have silver nor rum for Mister Hatcher.

But her relief overcame her misgivings.

Nonetheless, I shall be home, and Mister Hatcher's whip may flay Angus, not me.

- - - - -

In their quest of transport for Letticia, Hatcher rode

while Letticia walked behind, but Hatcher soon became aggravated by her sluggish pace, and he was about to call off their agreement when they came upon John Taggart and his assistant.

The two men were heading to St. Augustine on their way to Georgia, where their journey to Mosquito Inlet had begun, and Hatcher offered some of the same enticements to John as Lettie had offered to him, only he failed to mention the purse of coins and the extra bottles of rum.

Under the assumption that Hatcher would provide another gun in case of trouble and could help with the wagon on the road, John accepted the deal.

Lettie's ride to St. Augustine was secured, but after a few hours on the road, Hatcher's rum and his tolerance had nearly met their end, and he let it be known that he would ride on alone.

"Your travel is slow for my patience. In two days' time I'll be drinkin' rum with Angus. 'Twill take more 'n three for you to arrive," Then he tweaked one eyebrow to emphasize a warning to Lettie, "an' I'll be waitin' keen for my reward."

Lettie dared not argue, but the expansion of the compact worried her, and Hatcher's remarks added to her fright.

How might I gather food and rum enough for three men and Angus? I have only a few coins and two bottles of rum. If they be gone, I fear the price Mister Hatcher and these men will demand.

28.

The heavy rains of the summer had helped to raise the largest crop of squash and beans that Rafe and Noah had ever grown in their own fields. It was more than could be eaten, dried or stored by their families and friends before the next yield.

Ben's leg had improved, and although he needed a stick for support when he walked, he'd lent a hand in the harvesting and offered to sell the surplus in St. Augustine.

The day before the Stewarts and Coxes planned to make the trip home, their friends at the village were invited to come and commemorate the harvest with a feast. Many came, including the Native doctor.

The doctor was pleased with the healing progress of Ben's leg, but with concern, he recommended that Maya continue to confine herself to a bed or chair.

When he saw Ruth, a peculiar, though not wholly unfamiliar, feeling came over him.

"Are you well, Ruth?"

Hesitant to confide in him, Ruth dipped her head.

"I don't want tah worry Noah. I get tah thinking something ain't right, then I feel bettah, an' I put it from my mind."

"Noah will be happy," he smiled, "you carry his child."

With breathless excitement, Ruth repeated the doctor's prediction to Noah, and Noah lifted her up and spun her around as he kissed her and hugged her with more joy than he ever imagined he could feel.

When he set her down carefully, with respect for her condition, he announced the reason for his elation, and while he and Ruth cried with happiness, Maya and Rose wept joyously with them.

As the celebratory spirit escalated throughout the party, the music grew louder and the pulse became faster, and several of the reveling villagers removed strands of beads from around their own necks and placed them about the necks of Ruth and Noah.

Near nightfall, the feast came to an end, and the guests returned to their village with their carts full of squash and beans.

- - - - -

As clouds blazed a fiery orange at sunrise, Sam dismantled the oiled cloth tent from over Ben's wagon.

Under Ben's supervision, Noah, Sam and Rafe loaded the wagon for the journey to St. Augustine, and as the wagon filled, the sky cleared.

Sacks of beans hung over the top boards of the wagon and over the tarpaulin, which had been rolled up and tied to the side of the wagon.

Bushel baskets packed with squash were stacked high in the box, but a space had been left for Rose and Eyota and their bench, and the two chairs that Rafe had built for a guard at the city gate were tied to the back of the wagon beside the water barrel.

As Ben tested the straps and rigging, he seemed satisfied with it all.

"'Tis a goodly load. Heavier than any Henry has pulled before, but 'twill be no trouble for him and Amelia to draw together, not with the new harness and tongue that Rafe made. The wagon never looked better, and a fine sight we shall be as our horses strut side by side through the city gate."

Ben's snakebite notwithstanding, Rose was glad they'd come. She was thankful to have learned the truth about Maya's injury and that Jonathan had given Rafe food and water as a kindness even though it was against the wishes of Mister Hatcher.

Rafe and Maya's lenience had allowed Rose to think better of her son, but she worried for Maya, and leaving was difficult for her.

She prolonged her goodbyes until Maya reassured her.

"I'm most all well, Miz Rose, an' I'm grateful foh everahthin' you've done. I don't want you tah go, but you'll be back, and any money you bring from the market will be a blessin'. Be a good feelin' too if our crops could help feed the starvin' people in Mosquito Inlet. We know the awful sufferin' of hunger, an' the cruelty an' terror in livin' a slave. I thank the Lawd foh the life we have here, an' I thank the Lawd foh you. If you an' Mistah Ben hadn't taken me in when I came askin' foh help, I wouldn't have Rafe or Eli. I wouldn't have a life at all."

Rose surprised Maya with her own gratitude.

"'Twas a blessing for me that you chose my door. I had lost three daughters, and my sons had all grown and gone. I missed them all terribly and I missed being a mother. You filled that lonesome place in my heart, and because of you, I have learned to be a more understanding mother."

Their eyes moist with tears, Maya and Rose shared a wholehearted hug, and although they both found it hard to let go, Maya took a step back and smiled.

"You best go, Miz Rose. Mistah Ben be waitin', and Mistah Sam an' Eyota too, but the sun is climbin' a mighty blue sky an' it ain't waitin' foh nobody."

29.

Even though Rose had been reluctant to leave Maya and the baby, the journey home was pleasant and uneventful, and when the wagon made its entry into St. Augustine, a euphoric feeling stirred within Rose.

While they rode to the dock to speak with Jonas Wade the dockmaster, Rose shared her enthusiasm.

"Home! 'Tis good to be home! I love to see the masts of tall ships in the harbor and how the light reflects upon the water to paint the streets in changing shades. I have missed the bustling sounds of townsfolk as they run to do their errands or peddle their wares in the

J.S. Lavallee

square, and I have missed the smell of the bakery on the road to the gate and of the sea as the fishermen sell their morning's catch at the landing. There cannot be a better place to live than here."

Eyota merely smiled and nodded as she withheld her own sentiments.

This is Sam's home. His work is here, and I will love him here. I will go with him wherever he takes me and love him wherever he goes. I am proud I am his wife, but our visit has reminded my heart of my people and my cabin, and the children who play at the center of the village.

I have missed the quiet of the river and the peace in the forest and shaping pots beside a cove full with birds.

I have missed the music and the dances at our gatherings, and the stories our elders tell.

I wish, someday, Sam would make my village his own.

I know of no greater place to live than there.

While the women waited in the wagon at the landing, their husbands walked over to Jonas, but Ben and Sam's warm greetings were met with a brusque coolness which was uncharacteristic of the dockmaster.

"Gentlemen, I see that you are not here to work. When you both left at onest, you put me in earnest need of men and wagons to make deliveries."

"Yes," Ben began, "it could not be helped. We sent word that an unfortunate emergency called us away, but on the road I met a disagreeable snake who had

150

the audacity to bite me. My recovery caused our absence to be longer than we anticipated, but if our load can be sold today, I shall be here to make deliveries tomorrow. If you broker the sale, preferably with Doctor Turnbull, you will receive compensation."

With a nod, Sam concurred.

After strolling around Ben's wagon and estimating the worth of the crops, Jonas assured them,

"No doubt 'twill be a quick sale. Doctor Turnbull's settlement holds a hungry lot, and I'm told they be wearied of corn, but the doctor will surely pay with a note. It may take some time before the account is settled. There are traders here from other ports who may have money in hand."

Ben looked to Rose. She said nothing, but he knew her mind.

"Be the doctor in town?"

"I don't believe the doctor is here, but an agent of his keeps an office."

"We are newly arrived and have yet to view our properties. Our wives may seem patient, but they are wanting to be home. We can discuss this business when I return."

- - - - -

Given that Sam's wagon sat stored inside Ben's barn, the Stewart's small estate became their next destination, and as they trundled up the lane on their way, they passed the McGinn's house.

151

Weeds had grown in the garden, and a section of fence laid broken in the dirt along a side of the property, which alarmed Rose.

"The McGinn's be overgrown! Our own shrubs shall have grown the same, but Letticia McGinn would never allow her cow to breach its pen, nor vines to crowd her garden. Either they have moved away, or something untoward has happened. Letticia and I may have our differences, but I wish no ill for her or Angus. Please Ben, stop the wagon."

Sam stepped up to the door, but when his knock and his inquiry went unanswered, he walked around the property. Finding no one, he entered the house, and in a minute he came out.

"No one is here, but you are right, Rose, something has happened. The place is ransacked. The McGinn's have been robbed, or they've had quite a row. Someone in town will know what has come about."

- - - - -

When Ben walked back to the dock, Jonas had news.

"Your load can be sold to the doctor, but the offer is a paltry four dollars, and you would be expected to deliver it to his plantation. 'Tis a long way, farther than Fort Picolata by three and ten times the trouble, but two ships left for the Inlet this week past, and not a ship here is slated to sail south. If you accept the deal, you'll need another man or two. A courier brought news of a mutiny there, and angry men have escaped with guns. A reward of twenty dollars is offered for every runaway caught, but any fugitives will be hungry and desperate. You'll want a guard through the nights, and an extra eye through the days. A horse and wagon and a load of crops can be a great temptation for starving men on the run. With the woods full of Indian raiders and armed rebels from here to Mosquito Inlet, I cannot recommend the trip."

"Your warning is well taken, but I shall want to confer with Sam and Rose. Have you heard news of Angus McGinn or his wife Letticia? Our neighbors and their cow seem to be gone, and long enough for weeds to have grown."

"Aye, a disturbing story that, and the scandal has shaken the town. Constable Grimes has arrested Mister McGinn – for the murder of his wife."

30.

The damp, moldy corner of the dirt floor where he sat reeked of urine, likely that of both men and rats, and after a week, Angus still hadn't become used to the stench or the slick wetness of his clothing.

He'd adjusted to the shadowy darkness on his first day – better not to see the other men and the filth of the cell too clearly – but he'd lost track of what day it might be, and he marked time by when the tasteless mush was dispensed and when the waste pail was exchanged.

Not by choice, his imprisonment presented him with

sobriety. This new clarity of mind, along with the charges against him, began to change his way of thinking, and he ranted to the walls and the men he could scarcely see.

"I be a bloody fool! Were I na' a blighted drunk, my Lettie would ne'er have left me, but now the constable believes I've gone deranged and killed the woman! What have I done? Naught but drive her away by my own neglect. Lettie, where are you? Have you left me for some lovesick swain? I have none but myself to blame. You worked and cared and cooked for me while I did nothing. Nothing but sit in a tavern and drink. When you didna' come home, I should have gone to the constable, yet I cursed and searched for the money and rum I know you hide. I've been a terrible husband, while you've been a good wife."

Thoughts of a worse possibility haunted him, but he was loath to say the words out loud for fear the sound of them would make it true.

Has some depraved thief harmed you? I will make him pay! Has a heinous monster slain you? I will hunt the cur down!

Dear Lord, Lettie, dona' be dead!

With a grimy hand he wiped the seep of sweat from his face and neck, and begged,

"Forgive me Lettie, come home. I will do what chores you bid me do and treat you as the queen you are, and by my word, I'll ne'er drink a drop again."

31.

The pounding of hooves and the clinking of metal trappings could be heard before any horses could be seen, and Jonathan quickly led his own horse away from the road and further into the woods.

While he and Darian hid in an undergrowth of bushes, their breath attracted a bothersome swarm of gnats – just as a squad of British military on their way south passed by them. By reflex, Jonathan waved the pests away from his eyes, and the small British troop came to an abrupt halt on the leader's command.

Between the distance and the foliage, Jonathan could

see only fractions of the uniformed men and their horses, but he feared that his action had caused him and Darian to be spotted.

The men's voices were mere fragments of sound borne on the sweltering air, and Jonathan couldn't discern their words, but after a tense moment, the squad continued on their southerly path and a lone rider galloped his horse north.

As the horse and rider came closer to Jonathan, the man's lack of a uniform became apparent, and the identity of the steed became unmistakable.

Hatcher! He's come looking for us!

While Jonathan and Darian waited in the woods to gain distance between themselves and Hatcher, they tolerated the pestering gnats, and Jonathan rambled mostly to himself as he measured their alternatives.

"Our pretense might deceive the militia, but never Hatcher. If we go into Saint Augustine and Hatcher sees us, he will surely try to harm us or have us arrested. If we ride to a city other than Saint Augustine, the journey will take many days, but even if we are sparing, we have food and drink for only a day more. I could hunt, but the report of my gun could bring unwanted attention, as could the smoke of a fire, and to hunt would add days of time. We wouldn't have full canteens or the clothes we need for you to look like my wife and not an escaped servant, and riding for a week or more while carrying the two of us would be a severe strain on my horse. I could walk while you ride, but again, that would mean much more time. Whichever I choose, the risk is great."

Darian looked innocently into his eyes,

"I go where you go."

And feeling strengthened in her gaze, Jonathan made his decision.

"We shall ride to Saint Augustine. If we avoid the taverns, we might dodge Hatcher. My father and mother live in the city, and if they are there, I have hope that they will help us. Besides food and clothing, I can afford a wagon, which would make our journey safer and more comfortable. My father will know if there be one for sale."

- - - - -

The sun had begun to set when Hatcher arrived in St. Augustine, and the candle lamps in front of the public house where he'd met Angus McGinn were being lit by a lamplighter.

Tired and hungry and thirsty for rum, Hatcher entered the establishment, then gulped down a large flagon of beer before he demolished a bowl of stew and imbibed half a bottle of rum.

The aches from his long journey eased, his belly appeased, and his tongue well numbed, his speech slurred as he queried the patrons who shared his table.

"What man here has sheen Angush McGinn?"

He laughed, then drank another glug of rum.

"Ha! I've sheen his whysh. Bloody hell! That wench

be bold! Letticia McGinn says she be the besht cook in all the colonies. Right. Ish she? She shwore to give me coins an' rum an' supper – if I return her home. 'Tis the deal. I bri'g her home, an' Angush'll pay. The man shall trade his wealsh for the shrew, an' as yet, poor Angush doeshn't know!"

Hatcher stood up with his bottle in hand and swayed like a willow as he took a liberal swig, and the men in his company watched dumbfounded while he proposed a toast.

"To Angush! The mosht long-sufferin' fool I ever have met!"

As Hatcher raised his bottle in salute, he reeled backwards over the bench he'd been sitting on and collided with a serving maid. When the drinks she carried hit the floor, Hatcher came to rest with them and lay stupefied in the spill.

While the young maid collected the tankards, Hatcher offered no help nor said a word, nor did any of the other men, which provoked the girl.

"Sirs, have you no apology? 'Twas no fault of mine! I'll not lose my night's wage to this man's drunken bumbling. Someone must pay for the beer!"

Hatcher didn't stir an inch and the maid looked to his tablemates.

"Gentlemen, roust your ill-behaved friend, or bear his debt."

Faces almost as vacuous as Hatcher's gaped speechless, then one of the men recovered enough to respond.

"Send for the constable, and be quick, this man has kidnapped Letticia McGinn and holds her for ransom!"

32.

Hard-edged, shabbily dressed, and bristly unshaven, John Taggart and his man rarely spoke a word to each other, or to Letticia.

Although her own appearance and attire fared no better than theirs, Lettie felt wary of heading into the wilderness with the steely men, but eager to be home, she rode resolutely onward as she sat uncomfortably in the bed of the wagon.

After two days of travel the men seemed less daunting to her, and the three of them were content with their progress, until a board crumbled beneath the wagon as they crossed over a sparsely constructed bridge and a rear wheel fell into the wide hole.

John tried to push the wagon from behind while his assistant pulled on the horses' harness, but the wheel wedged tight in the gap.

When the wagon would budge neither forward nor backward, John asked Lettie to get down and provide a shoulder, but she flatly refused.

In the repressive heat, with the wagon at a rakish tilt, John's temper rose to rival Lettie's own, and a battle of wills ensued as their blaring voices reverberated through the forested swamp.

"Get down from my wagon, Missus McGinn! If you don't get down, I will throw you down! Right into the bloody river!"

"Mister Taggart, you are a crude, incompetent, and unreasonable man! We have agreed upon your fee for my carriage, and you shall be paid. I will not add labor to the toll!"

A web of purple lines wove across John's already reddened cheeks as he steamed,

"We won't be reaching Saint Augustine in this bloody wagon if you don't get down. Nay, you won't get there atall, Missus McGinn, if you don't get off of my wagon! Get off, before I feed you to the alligators below!"

"Mister Taggart! Where do you fancy that I should put my foot to get down? There be not a space beside this wagon on this narrow bridge. 'Twill be no need to toss me into the river for I shall be in it!"

"Come through to the back! You can get down from the back!"

"Through to the back, Mister Taggart? There be a stack of crates and a barrel in the back. I cannot make my way over the pile!"

"To the back, Missus McGinn, or I will come up there and throw you off to lighten the load!"

"Lighten the load! Oh, I can make the load lighter for you, Mister Taggart!"

Lettie shoved a box over the side, which splashed into the slow-moving water then bobbed a bit and sank, and before John could stop her, she triumphantly cast another crate overboard.

"Now you've done it, Missus McGinn, our rations are gone! Into the water with you!"

Lettie stood ready to fight, but despite her portly size, she was no contest for a man as big as John. He heaved her up and pitched her into the dark river, where, with her arms flapping feebly like ineffectual oars, she descended to the bottom like a canoe filled with water.

Although John felt no real remorse, and simply thought that Lettie had caused yet another problem, he jumped in after her.

When he hauled her out of the water and onto the river bank, she yelled at him in outrage, then went deathly silent as she stared at the painted faces of the Natives who peered at her from between the trees.

Not knowing whether the small group of men were

friendly or fierce, Lettie gave out a piercing scream, and the squad of British military riding south to Mosquito Inlet heard her faintly in the distance.

While Lettie and John and John's man stood motionless, fearing for their lives, the Native men walked to the wagon, carrying an arm thick branch between them.

The men chucked the branch between the spokes, and in one fluid motion, moved the wheel forward as they levered the wheel out of the crack. While the wagon rolled safely onto land, the Natives vanished into the woods, all to the astonishment of the three colonists, and done in the short time before the military troop arrived.

- - - - -

The troop's field officer knew John, for they'd frequented the same tavern in Savannah, and as he dismounted, he joked,

"John Taggart, my friend, was that your woman's wail we heard? What have you done, John?"

John laughed and parried back,

"The woman is unbalanced, gone mad from the heat. I found her bawling in the road, terrified of every beast and Indian imagined in her mind."

While the men spoke privately, Lettie tried to overhear, and although she caught just one word, she understood and feared its significance.

Reward! There be a reward for the doctor's runaway

servants!

The Natives' generous deed had rekindled the spark of compassion that Esteban had ignited in Lettie, and her plunge into the river along with her rescue reminded her of the young man's selfless heroism, but with this change in the tide, she worried that Mr. Taggart might return her to the doctor's plantation for money.

When John and the captain ended their conversation, the captain took his horse to be watered at the river, and Lettie went to John in the hope of making amends.

"I regret, sir, that I repaid your courtesy with the antics of a spoiled child. I behaved like common tripe, while people I believed to be beneath me risked their lives to help me, and proved themselves to be above me."

But John doubted her sincerity, and he scowled.

"There be a reward for any captured mutineers from Mosquito Inlet, but if you pay the increase of your fare, I'll not trade you for the reward."

"Increase of my fare, Mister Taggart? What is it you want?"

"The reward is twenty dollars."

The amount stunned Lettie.

"'Tis a considerable sum to equal. My cow would bring but ten, and though I cannot fault you for wishing to trade me for a reward, I am not a servant of Doctor Turnbull."

John shrugged his shoulders,

"Have a look at yourself, woman. No one will believe you, and from what I've seen, no one will care."

Lettie knew that to be true of the overseers at Mosquito Inlet, but possibly not of the military officer.

She took the chance and yelled,

"Captain! I am kidnapped! Mister Taggart holds me against my will and demands money for my release! Help me sir, I be a British citizen of Saint Augustine!"

John feigned indignation as he denied her allegation.

"My friend, it is as I told you. She has escaped from New Smyrna, and I'm taking her to the constable in Saint Augustine. A reward to be rid of the mouthy wench will be a right benefit."

The captain's grin revealed his bent toward John's version, which furthered Lettie's anger.

"'Tis no surprise to me to hear a kidnapper say such lies! Take me to the constable! Yes, by all means captain, take me to the constable. He knows me, and my husband."

After emitting a derisive snort, the captain reconsidered his opinion.

"Whom might you and your husband be?"

"I am Letticia McGinn, a citizen of good reputation, and my husband is Angus, Angus McGinn."

The change in the captain's attitude was immediate, and visible by his sudden stony pallor.

"Mister Taggart, you are under arrest!"

John began to protest, but the captain cut him short

and marshalled his troops, who had just completed their makeshift repair of the bridge.

"Tell your story to the constable. You've taken advantage of our acquaintance, and your corruption disgusts me."

The captain ordered one of his men to commandeer the wagon and fetter John in chains, then he expressed his concerns to Letticia.

"Missus McGinn, your husband is in jail, wrongfully accused of your murder, and we must save him from the gallows."

Seized with horror by the vision of Angus hanging from a rope, Lettie's face seemed to wither and age as the captain posed a question.

"Are you able to ride? I would send you to Saint Augustine post haste, on a company horse, with one of my men to protect you."

She hardly moved as she shook her head no.

"I have never sat on a horse leave ride one."

- - - - -

The slow wagon ride to St. Augustine gave Lettie time to reflect on her marriage, and as she envisioned a desolate life without Angus, she wavered between anger and anguish.

'Twas an awful suffering you've put me through, Angus, you deserve to fester in jail! Of what sort is the husband who would have his wife kidnapped?

But 'twas me who drove you to it, I know it, and 'twas

169

the rum that made you do it.

What man would not souse himself in rum that he might bear my reproach, my tirades and my selfish ways?

But while you drank in the taverns, you left me to do the chores alone, and I doused my loneliness with spirits at home.

I made your life miserable and I blamed you for my own unhappy life, and now, without a bit of proof, I've condemned you for my abduction.

Even if 'twas you who did the deed, perhaps I should not blame you.

I've been a mean tempered wife, but I will change.

Dear Lord, I don't want my husband to be hanged! Get me to Saint Augustine in time!

33.

Secluded in the forest a short distance from St. Augustine, Darian slept snuggled in Jonathan's arms while he lay awake, unable to sleep.

How can I ask Darian to come into the city with me? 'Tis a gamble, perhaps an unwise one, but I can't leave her in the woods alone.

If we pass through the gate in the morning without trouble, all will be well. Hatcher won't be about the streets early, and most of the town shall be either asleep or too busy to notice us.

If only Darian had suitable clothes.

The thought brought inspiration, and in the dawn, Jonathan helped Darian prepare for their entrance into St. Augustine.

While Darian knotted her hair and fixed her scarf to resemble a cap, Jonathan used his knife to cut the blanket into pieces.

As they gathered a portion of the cloth at her waist, they used a thin strip for a belt. They swathed another length around her shoulders, then crossed the wool over the front of her bodice and secured the ends at her back.

The primitively fashioned skirt and shawl hid much of Darian's torn and stained clothing, and gave her a much wider girth, but as she did a twirl, Jonathan admired her more than their handiwork.

"You look like a penniless peasant woman, but 'tis an improvement," he smiled, "and you are dressed in the proper mode for the city. We shall hope that you'll not be too closely inspected."

His horse's reins in hand, Jonathan walked while Darian sat to one side of the saddle, but as he led them toward St. Augustine, Darian's confidence faltered.

When she took in a nervous gasp, Jonathan reassured her,

"Give a smile, my pretty peasant. You are a beautiful pauper, and we shall get in safely."

- - - - -

Although the Stewarts and Coxes had hoped to help

feed the people at the doctor's plantation, after they weighed the risks and the days it would take to transport the load of squash and beans to Mosquito Inlet, they agreed that the venture would be too impractical, overly dangerous, and not something Maya would want them to do.

If there had been any men in the city willing to deliver the load to the inlet they would have charged twenty dollars or more, but Ben and Sam's own finances were negligible, and they had planned to give Rafe and Noah all of the profits.

When the two couples awoke to their first morning home, Eyota tended to her garden, Rose searched for the McGinn's cow and the chickens she'd set free when she left the city, and Ben and Sam sold the wagon load of squash and beans for eight dollars to a merchant at the landing whose ship would soon be sailing north.

While the merchant's crewmen emptied the wagon, Ben and Sam walked to the public house near the city gate, but as they approached the inn, they overheard one of the sentries at the gate having a minor dispute with a young couple who were attempting to enter the city.

"Sir, she is my wife." The young man expounded.

"My parents live here in the city, and we have come from Charles Town to stay with my father and mother. 'Twas a long and difficult journey, and our misfortune to encounter highwaymen on the road. They took most of our belongings, but 'twas luck for us that they did not find all of our silver," Jonathan gestured in the direction of Darian's padded stomach, "and a boon that they took pity on my wife and allowed us one of our horses."

Ben recognized the young man's voice, and both he and Sam were certain that the young woman had to be a servant from the New Smyrna Plantation and that Jonathan must have helped her to escape.

They strode lively to the gate, and as if they had rehearsed the scene, Ben's voice boomed.

"Son! You've come! And this lovely young woman must be your bride. Wonderful! Welcome home! Your mother will be pleased. She speaks of nothing else."

Ben gave his son a robust hug then scooped Darian down from the horse, and as he stepped between her and the guard, he put his arm around her and began to guide her into the city.

Sam took the reins from Jonathan (who had quickly caught on to the charade) and steered him and his horse away from the gate as he spoke loudly.

"Good to see you again, Jonathan. It has been some time hasn't it? Your mother spoke to me of your letter, and she has waited impatiently for you and your bride to arrive."

Then quietly, Sam told him, "We go to the landing. Your father's wagon is there."

Undone by the boisterous interruption, the guard glanced at the silver pieces that Jonathan had subtly laid in his palm, and with a shrug, he dropped the coins into his pouch and walked the other way.

- - - - -

When Rose couldn't find the McGinn's cow, she set out to catch her chickens. She found three of them and put them back in their coop, but while she combed the far end of their property for the fourth, she heard the rattle of Ben's wagon and the jangle of the horses' harness as they turned onto the lane.

She gave up the hunt to meet Ben at the stable, but while she crossed their small field, she could see that two people sat on the bench behind Ben and Sam. As they came closer, Rose's walk became a run, and she waved and yelled,

"Jonathan! Jonathan!"

Before the horses could be pulled to a stop, Jonathan jumped down and loped through the thigh high grass to meet her. As they embraced, she apologized.

"I should never have turned you away. I don't know how I could have done such a thing. Forgive me Jonathan."

And Jonathan eased her remorse,

"There is nothing to forgive, Mother. I'm grateful for your counsel. You made me see a worthier path, which gave me the will to rescue the woman I love. My Darian is here with me, come meet her."

Overwhelmed by her emotions, it had slipped from Rose's mind that another person had been sitting with Jonathan in the wagon, but when she saw the torn chemise and the crudely fitted wool skirt that Darian wore, she feared for the girl's safety.

"I am filled with joy to see you, and I shall love your Darian, but many townsfolk do not feel as kindly toward the new settlers as do your father and I or our friends. We must take her inside before the eyes of our neighbors encourage their tongues to wag. After Darian is bathed and wearing clean clothes there will be a bath and clothing for you, then you shall be fed, and when you are full, you shall tell us everything."

- - - - -

By the dim light of the candle in their small room, Ben and Rose dressed for bed as they debated over what might be the best plan for their son and Darian.

In an unusual turn, Ben became the more practical one when Rose fretted about the young couple's unmarried state.

"This be no time for a wedding, Rose. No one but Sam and Eyota must know that the children are here, not even the reverend. Our son loves the girl, he intends to marry her proper, and that is good enough for me. They have already spent nights together in the woods by necessity, and Jonathan tells me that he has married the girl in his heart. There be no need for them to sleep apart, let it be."

"You are right, husband. The poor girl is in need of Jonathan's comfort. When I helped her to bathe and dress, I saw how terribly thin and bruised she is. Her arms and legs bear the lash marks of a whip, her hands are badly cut from pulling roots, and her feet! Dear Lord, 'tis hard to be a witness of her suffering. I am reminded of the morning Maya came to our door and asked for transport. She was injured, afraid and starving. The young women have withstood similar trials, and they are both so brave. I am proud of our Jonathan for rescuing Darian."

Ben agreed entirely.

After a short discussion, he and Rose concluded that the best immediate haven for the young couple would be the village where Rafe and Maya lived. They feared that Rafe would not approve of the choice, but when Ben blew out the candle, they had no idea where else Jonathan and Darian could go or where they should go from there.

- - - - -

With respect for Rose's beliefs, Jonathan and Darian quartered inside the Stewart's barn, and while they lay on a bed of grass, the sound of a cat's purrs filled the darkness as the silky furred tabby kneaded a nest for itself beside Darian.

For the first time in months, Darian relaxed in a feeling of normalcy, but while she contentedly petted the cat, Jonathan thought anxiously about the next stage of their journey.

We need a wagon or a small cart that my horse can pull quickly, and we must leave as soon as we can, but where do we go? North? West?

To go west would be the most perilous. No, I won't take Darian to the West.

If we go north, we shall need to travel a far way to avoid being exposed, at the least, Charles Town.

Philadelphia might be best, my brothers may still be there, but to travel through a thousand miles of wilderness! I would not wish for Darian to endure it, nor for the two of us to undertake such a risky expedition.

To sail would be the safest – once we were aboard a ship – but we would be fools to attempt to board a ship in Saint Augustine or Savannah.

Bloody hell, this running away business is more difficult than I imagined when I first thought of it. I will never forgive myself if Darian is caught and sent back to Mosquito Inlet, or imprisoned in some ghastly, abominable jail.

34.

A prison guard unlocked the heavy door of a fetid cell, and as he wrested the door open, the trace of light that entered through the doorway revealed the wretched men inside.

The prisoners groaned and begged for food and pled for their release, but the jailers ignored their pleas and pushed Hatcher into the room.

Appearing to have been beaten, and still feeling the effects of his earlier excesses, Hatcher teetered a few steps, then tumbled to the floor.

As one of the jailers looked around, he spotted Angus

huddled in a corner, and he called out,

"Angus McGinn! You will come!"

A hush hung palpable in the air as the imprisoned men believed that Angus was headed for the gallows.

In the depths of hopelessness, Angus slowly raised himself up, and as he dragged his feet across the muck layered floor, he passed by Hatcher without either of them being aware of the other.

When the cell door shut behind Angus, the two guards each took an arm, and holding him firmly between themselves, they marched him to the constable's headquarters.

A tough and unyielding officer, Constable Grimes sat behind a well-ordered desk and on the only chair in the hot and sparingly furnished room, but he knew Angus, and he felt sorry for him as he acknowledged his presence.

"I won't prolong your misery, Mister McGinn."

The comment affirmed Angus's worst fear. As he pictured himself swinging from the beam of a gallows, his legs weakened and his body sagged, but the guards supported him, and the constable seemed to take no notice while he casually stated his facts.

"A kidnapper chose your wife for his prey, but the culprit is arrested and he will pay for his greed. He swears that Letticia is alive and well, and that, at this moment, she travels here by wagon from Mosquito Inlet. I see no reason to keep you, Angus. Go home and wait for your wife."

35.

Worn down from her long ordeal, Letticia McGinn
stood warily before Constable Grimes as he sat with his
elbows on his desk and his head in his hands.

Her tangled account of the events which had led to
the arrest of three innocent men had him frustrated,
but then, every exchange he'd ever had with her had
caused him either consternation or outright
infuriation.

Despite their history, he did his best to pacify her as
he tried to unravel her explanation.

"Your husband has been absolved from the charge of

your murder and sent home, Missus McGinn. Do not worry, I'll not arrest him for the conspiracy of your abduction, for as you say, there is no proof of his involvement. Since Mister Hatcher did not kidnap you, he will also be discharged."

With a snap of his fingers, the constable directed the two guards who stood by the entryway of his office to fetch Hatcher, then he returned his attention to Lettie.

"As for Mister Taggart. From what I understand, during his endeavor to transport you to Saint Augustine he became tempted by an offer of a larger reward than your own. I will not charge him for the contemplation of a kidnapping. However, I cannot trust that the man will respect the freedom of the citizens of Saint Augustine. The reward may persuade him to kidnap any of our people and take them to Mosquito Inlet. He will be asked to leave our city forthwith."

Lettie started to grumble her displeasure with John, but Constable Grimes chastised her.

"Be glad you are here, Missus McGinn, and that Mister Taggart has not signed a grievance against you!"

With some contrition, Lettie nodded in agreement, and the constable lowered the volume of his speech.

"Go home to your husband, and be grateful that he was not hung for your murder."

His business with Lettie concluded, Constable Grimes waved her away, but the two guards appeared in the doorway with Hatcher, and Lettie lingered out of curiosity.

One of the guards carried a sack filled with Hatcher's possessions, which he swung onto the constable's desk.

When the bag landed with a clunk, Grimes dumped out its contents then took a few coins from a small pouch in the pile.

"I trust that you will find your effects in order, Mister Hatcher, less the recompense for your keep and the stable of your horse. I do not expect an occasion to see you here again."

While Hatcher gathered his possessions, coiled his whip, and took his rifle from the guard, Grimes spoke a final word to Lettie.

"'Twas Mister Hatcher's testament that saved your husband."

Lettie looked at Hatcher with wide-eyed surprise.

"Sir, my husband and I are indebted to you, and I owe you the suppers I promised to cook for you."

"I have need of a good meal, Missus McGinn, but I'll not be fit for one till I've found a bath."

"Come with me, Mister Hatcher, I shall warm the water for your bath, and Mister McGinn can thank you for his life."

36.

While Rose baked the day's biscuits outside in her brick oven, the rising sun gilded the clouds with brilliant gold, and the dazzling display reminded her of how much she loved the early mornings of St. Augustine.

Grateful to have her son under her roof, if only for a time, she put her worries aside and set a table inside the house with her finest marmalade, smoked fish, and special for the occasion, tea.

The four of them ate in polite silence, then Jonathan reopened a previous conversation.

"I agree with you, Father. Your friend's village sounds to be the best shelter for us, and a good place to build a cart, but a safe departure from this city may near be impossible."

Taken aback, Ben chortled a little, then after a moment, he replied,

"Two years ago, I built a hidden compartment under my wagon. We haven't used it since then, but it would hold Darian, if she can abide a small, dark space for a time. The space is the width of the wagon bed, but 'tis quite shallow. We once hid Maya there, to conceal her from bounty hunters and smuggle her through the city gate. The trick went well, and a few miles west of the city we stopped and got her out. We could do the same for Darian. Would you do that Darian?"

Darian questioned Jonathan with her eyes, and when he nodded, she smiled at Ben.

"I do what you ask."

Ben extended the plan.

"If Sam will come with us, three men on a hunt for deer should be able to get through the gate without a search, and 'twill be an advantage to have Sam with me on the way back."

Although Rose felt disappointed, she understood.

"I shall wish for the time I would have spent with my children, but I want all of us to be safe."

- - - - -

Confident that all would be well and that Sam would

be willing to travel with him, Ben whistled a tune while he walked down the lane toward Sam's, but when he came to the McGinn's house he heard a whistle compliment his own, and Angus came out onto his stoop.

Wearing a satisfied grin, Angus breathed in a lungful of air, and savored it as if it were perfume.

"Ah, good day, Mister Stewart. 'Tis a fine day for a tune, and a good day to be in one's home."

"'Tis that, Mister McGinn, good day. Missus Stewart and I have noticed your absence, and that of Mistress McGinn's. You are well, sir?"

"Ne'er better."

"And your wife, Angus, be she in good health as well?"

Angus stepped down from the stoop and into the lane to speak more personally.

"Aye, she's a changed woman, Ben. She returned home to me afternoon past, a delight, I swear it. 'Twas a kidnapping what changed her. A terrible experience she had. Snatched and shipped off to Mosquito Inlet, kept as a slave in that swamp, 'twas a dear lesson for her. I'm a new man meself, having sworn off the drink. Constable Grimes had me molding in jail, charged with my wife's murder! Lucky for me, an overseer from the doctor's plantation rescued Letticia and saved my neck from the noose. He lodges here with us, and he's welcome to stay as bloody long as he likes."

The word "overseer" sliced fear through Ben like an

arrow, and pained him with the urgent need to warn his son, but Angus prattled on.

"The constable released me from that filthy sty early yester morn. I scrubbed myself pink till I rid myself of the stink, then slept through the day in bed. My own bed! The bliss of it! The gallant soul who saved me sits at my table, and Lettie is bent on adding twenty pounds onto him. Lord, let her put thirty pounds on him! The smell of her cooking is heaven, to dine on it divine!"

Ben tipped his hat, "I celebrate with you, Angus, but I must get on, I have an errand which needs be done. Good day to you, my friend."

But as Ben started to leave, the McGinn's door opened, and in the doorway, Hatcher leaned against the door jamb.

Ben recognized him instantly, and the shaft of that fearsome arrow almost staked Ben to the ground.

A suspicion that they'd met in the past crossed Hatcher's mind, and he squinted as he tried to recall, but Ben tipped his hat again to partially mask his face and hurried on his way before an introduction could be made.

At the end of the lane, Ben made sure that the two men couldn't see him, for rather than turn toward Sam's, he circled around to the far side of his property and sprinted back to his house.

Out of breath, he gushed his news as he entered through the rear door.

"We have trouble! Mister Hatcher is at the McGinn's! They have taken him in! Our name has surely been spoken between them and he's bound to come prowling about. He could be here at any minute. We must hide the children and Jonathan's horse and get them out of the city. None of us are safe."

Often at her best in a crisis, Rose set her nimble mind to work.

"We shall all leave for the village. I do not wish to deal with Mister Hatcher or Constable Grimes alone. Jonathan, you and Darian must both hide under the wagon, and at once. 'Twill be a tight fit and a long time to spend hampered into a shallow nook, but if a person comes looking, you shall not be found, nor shall you be seen when we ride by the McGinn's or go through the city gate."

When no one voiced an objection, Rose went on.

"Help them into the cuddy, Ben, and tamp the plank down. Ride Jonathan's horse to Sam's barn, but take the back foot path to avoid the McGinn's, then walk the same route home. 'Twould be less bother if that path had room for our big wagon, but I shall cover the floor of the box with hay and pack the necessities while you are gone. With the young ones tucked beneath the bed, we shall drive up the road to Sam's where we can harness Jonathan's horse to the wagon beside Henry. If we are careful and act with haste, Mister Hatcher will never see Jonathan's horse nor the children, and we shall be out of the city within the hour."

- - - - -

As Ben bent to set the last board down above Jonathan and Darian, he heard a noise behind him.

Henry neighed and shook his head to show his agitation, and with a terrible sinking feeling, Ben felt certain that someone was watching.

Mister Hatcher must be here. What has he seen?

Ben straightened up to prepare for a confrontation, but as he turned to face Hatcher, the person he saw posed beside the wagon was Letticia McGinn.

With her hands on her hips, she spoke frankly.

"I know what you are up to, Mister Stewart."

At her words, Ben felt his heart thump, and his mind filled with scenes of arrests and disaster, but the lump that formed in his throat kept him from speaking.

Lettie saw the fright in his eyes, and she knew that her past had earned her that look.

"There be no need to fear me, Ben, I've come to help you and to warn you. 'Tis a Mister Hatcher you must fear. At my home this evening past, in the fever of a drunken stew, Mister Hatcher raved about a man named Jonathan and a runaway girl from Mosquito Inlet. He said that when he finds them, he will kill them. I learned this morning that the Jonathan he pursues is your son. I want no harm to come to you or your son or the girl, but I neither desire injury for Mister Hatcher. Angus and I owe him our lives. He saved Angus from the gallows, and he rescued me from

Doctor Turnbull's vile plantation. I suffered the torture forced upon the servants and slaves there, and I have seen terrible cruelty, starvation, and sickness. One of those poor, pitiable souls helped me at the risk of his life, and I would help any one of them to escape if I could."

Even though Angus had boasted of the change in his wife, Ben had doubted it. To see this new Lettie with his own eyes stunned him. He cleared his throat and meekly asked,

"What would you have me do, Letticia?"

"'Twas your son and the girl I saw from my window yester afternoon, I'm sure of it, and I see a horse in this stable that I believe does not belong to you. I think you harbor the runaways, but they must find some other place to hide. This morning I fed Mister Hatcher more food than any two men should eat at one meal, and I poured enough rum into his cup to drop three. 'Twas all the rum I had, and most of my larder, but at this moment, Mister Hatcher sleeps like a bear. When he awakes he will come here, for before he lapsed into his hibernation, he remembered that you be the father of the Jonathan he seeks."

Amazed by her transformation and touched by her consideration, Ben didn't let on that he knew about Hatcher, but with discretion, neither did he reveal that the young couple hid underneath his wagon's floor.

"Thank you Lettie. You have become a worthy friend, and I shall heed your advice."

37.

When Letticia helped Hatcher to drink himself into oblivion, she averted his threat for the Stewarts, which eliminated the necessity for Ben to take Jonathan's horse to Sam's by the back path.

As Ben rethought the plan, he reasoned that there was also no need for Jonathan's small horse to pull the wagon beside his substantially larger draft horse.

He hitched Henry to the wagon, tied Jonathan's steed to the back, and boldly drove his family right down the lane and past the McGinn's.

With the additional time afforded to them, Ben

stopped at Sam's to tell him about their scheme, and Sam offered his help.

"Eyota and I will come with you. I have friends who have a homestead near Fort Picolata, and they may provide a safer path to the North than Jonathan could devise on his own. They might be able to send your son and Darian to friendly households on the way, and arrange a guide to lead them through the more dangerous corridors."

Traveling in two wagons, both families feared for what the guard might find, and worried that Hatcher might turn up at the city gate to foil their plans.

They hid their anxieties well while the guard questioned them, and when he began to look over Ben's wagon too thoroughly for comfort, Ben distracted him with a convenient lie.

"Sir, I am commissioned to deliver the horse behind my wagon to Picolata. The seller got a good price for him, and I am promised a tithe for his delivery, but the little thing could never draw a full wagon nor work a hard day in the field. Might they be assembling a race, sir? I believe I overheard something about a race. I think the horse could win one. 'Tis a fine steed, is it not, sir?"

The guard walked back and rubbed the horse's neck, then stroked a forearm and smiled as he felt the smoothness of the mount's buttocks.

"I do enjoy a fast race. I believe my horse would best him, yet 'twould be a good run."

Then he stepped aside to allow the wagons to pass.

- - - - -

Although the summer sun bore down on them, the Stewarts and Coxes tolerated the heat and welcomed the dry weather, for opposed to their previous trip, the firm dirt of the road made for easy travel.

When they'd gone far enough from the city to stop safely, they released Jonathan and Darian, and they laughed about how easily Ben had fooled the guard.

With good weather and willing horses, the company reached the Picolata farm of Sam's friend, Boyd Lawson, in seven hours, and Boyd greeted them with a kind welcome.

After introductions, Boyd suggested that they camp with their wagons in the barn or behind it, whichever they would like, and Sam and his old friend went into the farmhouse to talk.

Over tankards of beer they traded all the news they had with either joviality or sober astonishment, depending on the subject under discussion, but when they got to the business of escape, Boyd was straightforward.

"I can write a letter of introduction for them, and I can draw them maps of the routes they should take, but they will have to remember where the safe houses are and the names of those who will help them, as I shall not write that down. 'Twould be a hardship and very dangerous for them to ride inland all the way to

Philadelphia. 'Twill take nigh on two weeks just to reach Charles Town in a cart, but I have good people in that city. They could help them to secure passage on a ship or find a new home there. If Darian could ride a horse, the trip would take half the time, and be the better to cross rivers and streams."

Sam looked pensive. "There may be a post out on them and a reward."

"Their names need be changed 'tis all. Jonathan could be Ethan, or Aedan. Hmm, and Darian? An unusual name, and too memorable if anyone might read a post or hear the name. She should be Anna. Simple, common. Ethan and Anna Stewart. No, Aedan and Anna Stevens. Yes, I shall write those names in the letter."

Sam said the names aloud and approved.

"You'll want money. How much will it be?"

Boyd threw his head back and laughed,

"Nothing for me, and more than the lad will want to spend for ship's fare, but far less than 'tis worth. I shall do the work this night, and they can be off on the morn. There's a farm about forty miles north of here where they can rest safely for a night, and they can cross the river about twenty miles above that, at a spot where cows are forded. For tonight, you will all be safe here and well fed. We have no lack of food this year, and as you know, my wife enjoys entertaining guests, of whom she says we have too few. That said, shall we see what my wife is cooking? The aroma coming from her kitchen is making me hungry."

- - - - -

While the day had brought an undemanding ride, the night presented a million stars to sleep beneath, and although Jonathan and Darian chose to sleep in the loft of the barn, Ben and Rose and Sam and Eyota made their beds outside in their wagons.

In awe of the enormous sky filled with so many tiny specks of light, Rose lay close to Ben as she gazed at the heavens and pondered over the new direction that their lives had taken.

"Everyone and everything has changed, though I think it be mostly for the better. Letticia is improved, and I am glad for the change in our Jonathan. None of us can avoid disappointment or the sadness that comes with tragedy, but even those have become altered in a moment of joy. Maya and Rafe have a son, Noah and Ruth shall soon have a child, and Jonathan has blessed us with another daughter. We too have changed, my husband, but I wonder if we be the better for it. I feel guilty for the little lies we have learned to tell so effortlessly."

Endeared by her heart, Ben fondly smoothed a wisp of her hair.

"Do not worry, Rose, we mean no harm. The little pretenses we make are honorable deceptions, for we desire to save lives by them. I believe we are forgiven for such tales, and perhaps we are praised for them."

With the charm of his persuasive smile, Ben gave her cheek a kiss, and teased,

"I would never lie to you, Rose."

38.

Hatcher awoke slowly, still groggy from his over indulgences of the morning. Any movement he made nauseated him, as if he tossed on a ship, seasick in a violent storm.

Eyes half open, his vision unclear, he tried to determine the time of day.

Gradually, the reason for his ailment came to him.

Ah yes, rum. Rum and Letticia McGinn.

"Rum." He mumbled to the room as it seemed to spin around him.

A little louder he asked, "Missus McGinn?", then he

regretted it.

Bloody hell, my head. Where is the woman?

Angus had gone into the streets of town to search for Lettie's cow, and while Lettie weeded and pulled vines in her garden, she wished that Mister Hatcher would just go away.

Alone in the house, Hatcher rolled himself out of the chair in which he'd been sleeping, and lurched through the door as his belly convulsed.

Lettie stood not more than twenty feet from where he emptied the contents of his stomach, and she seized on the incident.

"Mister Hatcher! Shame on you, sir! When I invited you into my home, I was not aware that you are a drunkard. You must learn to conduct yourself suitably. I cannot permit this sort of behavior in my house. 'Tis time for you to leave."

Hatcher spit and wiped his mouth on his sleeve, and gave Lettie a serious, incredulous stare.

"You must learn to honor your word, Missus McGinn. I will have the full payment of our contract."

"I have given you everything I have, and it seems that you have not valued it. You've gorged yourself on the two excellent meals that you were promised, and you have guzzled down two bottles of the finest rum to be had. There is nothing more here than the few vegetables that are left in my garden."

While Letticia held her temper to a simmer, Angus appeared down the lane, and as he slowly sauntered home, he led her cow with a rope.

Although Lettie was pleased to see that her cow had outlasted its abandonment, the timing of the animal's return was less than favorable, for Hatcher had also seen Angus and the cow, and he gave Lettie an angry ultimatum.

"If you cannot make good on your pledge, I will have your cow."

"My cow! What would you do with my cow?"

Hatcher's limber brow lifted with his harsh retort, "Madam, I would eat it!"

Brought to her boiling point, Lettie exploded.

"Leave my property! Go at once! You have drunk all the rum, the meat is eaten, and the money is spent. You have been bathed, your horse has been fed, and our agreement is met. You shan't have my cow! Get your bag, get on your horse, and be gone!"

"You owe a fair purse an' two more bottles of rum before we're square. I will have satisfaction."

"There be no silver here nor rum, and you will not have my cow! Now go!"

Hatcher would have gone for his whip, but Angus was nearly home, and the day was well into afternoon.

As he faced Lettie, the neighboring house stood in view behind her, and the sight reminded him that the house belonged to Jonathan's father.

Never a patient man, Hatcher took the last word.

"You waste my time. I have better things to do 'n squabble with a woman."

- - - - -

A few roaming chickens scattered out of the way and squawked their annoyance at the intrusion as Hatcher walked into the Stewart's barn with his horse.

He'd gone to the Stewart's house first, but no one was home, and their absence had irritated him.

While he explored the stable, his horse ate from a small pile of hay, but when he found no one there either, his own hunger added to his aggravation.

He rode back down the lane as he headed for a tavern, and Lettie watched him from a window while he passed by her house.

Would that we were rid of Mister Hatcher, but I expect he'll creep back in the night like a hungry rat. He has a thirst to find the Stewart's son and an appetite for my cow, but he'll not find the Stewart's son and he'll not have my cow.

39.

The small tavern that Hatcher chose served only a thin soup for meals, which through the day became thinner as the soup was watered down regularly to stretch the pot, but the beer, rum and whiskey were strong and in good supply, and Hatcher helped to reduce the potent inventory with enthusiasm while he complained loudly about the soup to the few patrons in the room.

"'Tis the gutter sluice that be fed to the indents an' slaves at Mosquito Inlet! The cook here has no tongue to taste with. No tongue at all! Now, there be a woman in this town with a tongue so sharp she wields it like an ax, but the wench is clever with food, an' her soup is appealing to the tooth. Perhaps one of you has heard of the wife of Angus McGinn."

"Letticia McGinn." An unsavory looking character groused into his beer.

"The woman be known to me and to most of the people in this city. I've heard no rumors about her cooking, but her reputation rests on that tongue of hers. There be no man here who hasn't felt pity for Angus."

Hatcher eyed the gristly fellow and wondered if he might be agreeable to his purpose.

"Allow me to buy you a drink, sir. What be your pleasure, beer, rum, whiskey? Come, have a seat. Call me Hatcher an' tell me more."

"Dugal be my name, friend, and rum be my liking when I'm not the one buying, but I haven't much to tell."

Then he chuckled, "I know that Letticia McGinn lie drunk on this floor not a month ago, and as a charity to Angus, a crew of seamen sent her off in a barrel! On the first ship leaving the harbor!"

A good laugh came easily to them both, then Hatcher maneuvered toward his objective.

"I believe that ship sailed to Mosquito Inlet, for 'twas there I rescued Letticia from an unfortunate fate. When I arrived here in Saint Augustine, I found Angus in jail, set to hang for her murder, an' I saved his ruddy neck from the noose."

With high regard, and a lean to his liquor, Dugal raised his cup.

"You, sir, be a champion among men."

In a quieter voice, Hatcher spoke more discreetly.

"Letticia pledged a generous reward for my service, but after I saved her and her husband, she claimed to have only a cow with which to pay me, an' now she refuses me the cow. Her debt exceeds the worth of her cow, yet I would have the cow an' forgive the balance. Would you not do the same?"

"I am of the mind that Letticia should pay her debt. She should be thankful for your valor and your willingness to accept the cow. You are a prince."

Pleased with his new ally, Hatcher traded flattery as he gestured to the barkeeper for two more drinks.

"Dugal, you are a gentleman, an' you are right. The woman is ungrateful, an' as you say, she should pay."

"Perhaps, if you spoke with Angus."

"Ah, the poor man be no match for his wife an' her bloody ax, an' I have no time to deal with the matter; I am engaged in a search for a man named Stewart."

"Be the Stewart you seek Benjamin Stewart? I know of none other. I've loaded his wagon many times at the landing, and this morning on my way to the bakery, I saw him and his wife in his wagon as they left the city. I heard him say to a guard that he delivers a horse to Fort Picolata."

"My good friend! You have saved me an amount of

205

time an' trouble, an' I'll be off with the dawn, for this night be better spent without a ride to Fort Picolata. Have you a barn, Dugal? Do you butcher? I have no place to keep a cow, an' I would sell it, but your recount merits a return. Help me collect my cow tonight, an' the beast is yours to do with as you will."

- - - - -

By the time Hatcher and Dugal left the tavern, low clouds obscured the streets in muffled darkness and suffocated the city with heat. No stars or moon shone through the muggy blanket, and Hatcher was glad for it.

Their cunning alliance made, the two men walked the dark and murky lanes to the McGinn's, and while Hatcher led his horse, a very willing Dugal listened to Hatcher's plan.

"'Tis a night well fit for takin' what's rightly ours, for the fog makes a useful partner. The McGinn's fence be a feeble pen of sticks an' boards, an' easy enough to remove a share from the rear side of the pasture. Before Letticia discovers that her debt is paid, the cow will be slaughtered to roast, an' I'll be halfway to Picolata."

Leaving his horse at the back fence, Hatcher sneaked his way through the small field behind the McGinn's house. Dugal followed closely, with rope in hand.

Their outlines made vague by the mist, the pair had convinced themselves that they could abscond with

206

the cow undetected, but neither of them had considered Letticia's tenacity.

Lettie had tethered her cow near her back door stoop, and while she waited outside for Hatcher, she sat on the step with her hand on the long handle of the flat iron pan beside her.

As her wait dragged on into the night, she nodded drowsily, and she'd almost given up the watch, when through the haze she spied Hatcher.

The fog also helped to hide Lettie, and while Hatcher stood unwittingly as he worked to cut the cow's rope, Lettie whacked his head with the pan. When Hatcher landed on the ground, she shouted for Angus.

Dugal stood at the other side of the cow, but with the sound of the pan against Hatcher's head and the thud Hatcher made as he met the ground, Dugal suspected that they'd been caught. With Lettie's yell, he was sure of it.

He ran in a drunken fright back through the pasture, gripped the reins of Hatcher's horse, and although a bit clumsily, rode away as if his life depended on it. Which it may have.

When Angus came out, Hatcher seemed lifeless, and Lettie had him fettered hands to feet.

"Best get the constable, Angus," she said smugly, "I won't be feeding Mister Hatcher again."

- - - - -

Trussed like a pig prepared for the spit, Hatcher

spent the remainder of the night oblivious to the world as he lay in the dirt behind Lettie's house.

Sometime after sunrise a boot to his buttocks roused him, and Hatcher's first wakeful breath of the morning air insulted his nostrils with the caustic fumes of fresh cow dung.

He cursed at the smell and the ropes that bound him, but the hammering of his headache abruptly muzzled him.

He looked up, expecting to see Lettie, but the assault had come from Constable Grimes, and the constable's unsympathetic expression did not bode well for Mister Hatcher.

Hauled off to the jail in Grimes cart, Hatcher's dry flask and his almost empty purse hung from his belt, but his horse, rifle and whip did not go with him.

As things were, he didn't have enough money or assets to buy or barter his way out of punishment, and in Grimes office, Hatcher made an effort to regain his belongings.

"I would add a good rifle to my silver if you would allow me to get my horse from Letticia McGinn."

Constable Grimes kept a stern face as he shook his head no.

"Missus McGinn does not have your horse or your possessions."

At first surprised, it then occurred to Hatcher that Dugal must have taken them, and he didn't want to implicate Dugal, just find him.

His only recourse was to convince Grimes that he was innocent.

"A debt is owed to me by Letticia McGinn, a reward promised for her rescue, but she was unable to pay the agreed upon amount an' she proposed her cow as compensation. Although the cow's worth did not meet the size of her debt, I felt sorry for the poor woman an' I decently accepted."

But the constable had already formed his opinion.

"Missus McGinn contends that she furnished you with meals and a bed and more, but you drank heavily and behaved badly, and she evicted you from her property, at which point you threatened to take her cow. She says the rope around the neck of her cow has been cut with your knife."

"The woman lies and tries to cheat me."

"Don't bother to deny it, Mister Hatcher. I know you are a drunkard and I know the knife is yours. It sat here on my desk with the rest of your property two days ago. You have proven yourself to be the liar, and you will be punished for the attempted theft of Missus McGinn's cow."

Hatcher started to dispute the accusations, but Constable Grimes stopped him and gave orders to the guards.

"A cell for Mister Hatcher. Where he can wait for his reward."

40.

Outside of the jail in St. Augustine, at the hottest part of the day, a small crowd of townsfolk watched with enjoyment while two guards stripped Hatcher of his shirt and shackled his arms to a whipping post.

Attached with chains to the stout wood post, the metal cuffs had baked in the sun and they seared Hatcher's wrists, but the guards ignored his yelp, and Constable Grimes chose not to hear as he walked to his office.

While the two guards took turns with their whips they held back no force. Within a couple of minutes

Hatcher had endured six lashes, and he could no longer hold himself up.

Hanging by his wrists, dripping sweat and blood, he let out a scream in agony, but four more strokes were slowly counted before his ordeal ended.

On his release from the post, Hatcher moaned and collapsed to the ground, and the two guards dragged him back inside the jail, where they dropped him like a bag of meat at the feet of Constable Grimes.

"I have been lenient, Mister Hatcher, due to your employ by Doctor Turnbull, and you have received only half of the lashings that might have been levied upon you. I have also spared your shirt, which will save you some inconvenience."

The constable almost smiled as he threw the shirt at Hatcher.

"When you are able to stand, my men will escort you to the gate."

A pitiful lump, his back stinging with pain, Hatcher drew himself up to hunch over his knees, and spoke with difficulty as he begged.

"Sir, my horse. I must have my horse before I can leave the city."

Grimes knew that there was more to the story.

"What man has your horse, Mister Hatcher? Missus McGinn believed that you had another man with you. Out with it, or shall I have my men complete the other half of your whipping?"

Hatcher hadn't expected the additional interrogation.

Bloody hell. I can't tell him the truth. If I betray Dugal, he'll cut out my tongue, an' if the men at Mosquito Inlet hear of it, they'll slice up what's left of me.

If I lie to Grimes, an' he learns the truth, I'll never get out of this jail alive.

That could be the worst of the two, but I won't leave my horse to Dugal, nor give him my rifle an' whip.

"A man named Dugal might have him."

"How is it that he would have your horse?"

"While we drank in a tavern we talked well into the night, an' the rum may have affected my reason, but I offered him the cow. He believed the cow to be mine, for I believed it myself, and as I meant to leave the city at dawn, we went to collect the beast. Dugal must have ridden my horse home when I was struck."

"You would have me believe that the two of you prowled in the night and cut a cow's lead because you owned the cow? No, Mister Hatcher, do not think me a fool, you snuck in the dark to steal the animal."

The criticism brought forward a memory for Hatcher, a recollection in which the constable had deemed Lettie to be unhinged, and Hatcher made use of the term.

"Letticia McGinn is unhinged. If not her deceit, then at best her misunderstanding. The woman is completely mad. After I settled for the cow I left her property an' told her that I would be back for the creature. I'm sorry I ever helped the woman."

Since the constable had said the same about Lettie

and had lamented their every encounter, doubt sprouted in his mind from the seed, and he began to think that he would also come to regret this instance.

"If Mister Dugal has your horse, that would confirm his participation, in which case, he could be flogged at the post. However, if he tells a like story, he might absolve you both."

Weak and unsteady, Hatcher remained on his knees and worried whether Dugal would expose his half-truths or back him.

"I don't know where he lives. I only know the tavern where we met."

Grimes supposed that Hatcher was stalling.

"I am familiar with Mister Dugal and his residence."

"My horse, will I have my horse?"

"I shall see what Mister Dugal has to say."

With a flick of his hand, the constable summoned a guard.

"Take him back to his cell."

41.

When the succession of almost daily storms ended, the scorching sun parched the soil, and after a week of drought, activities in the Native village slowed to a near halt as many inhabitants spent their time at the river while they sought relief from the soaring temperatures.

In the first light of the hot morning, Rafe and Noah walked to the riverbank to fish, but alone with her child in the cabin, thoughts of the river's cool water tempted Maya beyond her capacity to resist.

When Ruth came to visit after sunrise, Maya made a

request.

"I miss the rivah. There be somethin' special 'bout sittin' by that watah. Even the night can't rid us of this heat, but the rivah can. I want tah go there, Ruth, come with me. I'll carry Eli, an' we can watch our men catch dinnah."

"The doctah says you shouldn't walk fah, an' you musn't be carrying Eli neithah. I'll bring some watah from the well foh you. That will cool you."

With an impish grin, Maya chided,

"Truly, I'm well. Come with me or I'll haftah go without you."

Concerned that Maya might be serious, Ruth insisted,

"No, Maya, wait heah while I get Rafe an' Noah. Rafe can carry you tah the rivah, an' Noah can carry Eli. I won't be gone long."

When the wait seemed long to Maya, she slung a cloth around herself and swaddled Eli into it, then she set out for the river path, but at the edge of the garden she lowered her son to the ground.

"Goodness Eli, when did you get so heavy?"

When the men and Ruth returned, they saw Eli crawling in the garden, and not far from him lay Maya.

Rafe was the first to realize that Maya wasn't just asleep. His heart pounded as he ran to her, but it felt to him as if his feet were weighted and slow to move, and tears began to wet his cheeks.

As Rafe carried her to their cabin, Noah took off in a

run to get the village doctor, and Ruth clutched Eli in a panic as she followed Rafe and cried,

"Oh Lawd, Rafe, I nevah shouldah left her. I don't know what I was thinking. She said she would wait, she said she felt well, but I know she be strong willed. I nevah shouldah gone. Please Maya, please wake up. I'm so sorry, Rafe."

"There be no blame for you, Ruth, or for Maya. I'm the one who went fishin', but none of us could have known this would happen. She seemed well."

As Rafe laid Maya on the bed, Ruth put Eli into his basket, but with loving concern, Ruth hovered over Maya and touched her forehead.

"Deah Lawd, she's on fire, but she's shivering with cold. I'll get her a blanket."

While Rafe held Maya's limp hand between his own leathery palms, he spoke to her softly.

"All my life I've loved you, Maya. From the time I was five an' you were three, I knew I would always love you. You were just a kit, an' I was barely more than a cub, but I knew, an' I knew you loved me too. You gave me the will to endure this world, an' you gave me my name. You were such a little thing, you couldn't say Ralph. It came out Rafe. From that time on, I was Rafe. I was your Rafe, an' I will always be your Rafe. Stay with me, don't go. Stay here with me an' our beautiful son. We love you, Maya, we love you so much."

Ruth gently spread a quilt over Maya, the one that Rose had sewn and given unfinished to Maya and Rafe as a wedding present, and Rafe continued his loving serenade.

42.

Filled with hope and fellowship, and only an occasional thought of Hatcher, the Stewarts and Coxes arrived at Maya and Rafe's cabin after a congenial and beneficial visit with Sam's friend Boyd.

When no one greeted them, Hatcher became Ben's first thought, and he cautioned everyone to stay in their wagons.

While Sam held his gun at the ready, Ben shouted out,

"Rafe! Are you there?"

But it was Noah who came out of the cabin, and lines

of worry creased his face.

"You gottah wait out heah. The doctah be removin' the bullet from Maya. He says theah be no othah choice."

The time crept slowly by before the Native doctor came out of the cabin, but when he appeared he gave a nod to Ben, and without a word or a smile, he and his apprentice jumped up on their horses and rode away.

At their silence, Rose felt her hope for Maya begin to slip away, but Ben made a lighter observation.

"Maya lives, or the healer would have told us. Come, we should go inside."

Drained to exhaustion, Rafe met them at the door.

"Maya sleeps an' barely breathes, but she is alive. The doctah has given me a slivah of hope, an' I'm prayin' harder than I evah have in my life."

With sympathy, Ben grasped him in a hug.

"We pray with you, Rafe, but the village doctor is a modest man. If he says there is hope, she will live. I myself can attest to his skill and humility."

Although Rose wavered between hope and hopelessness, she soothed Rafe with the words of encouragement that she wanted to believe.

"Surely, now that the bullet has been taken, Maya's wound will heal and she will be well."

As Rafe thought about Maya, he looked out from his cabin.

Sam and Eyota and a young woman lingered near Ben's wagon – and with them stood Jonathan.

Every muscle of Rafe's body tensed in anger as he struggled against his desire to strike Jonathan.

How do I welcome Ben's son into my home, when a few feet from where he stands, Maya might be dyin'? Jonathan isn't blameless for her sufferin'. He helped Hatcher put us both through hell.

It be one thing to tell a mother that her son did a kindness once, but how do I believe that he isn't a bad man when not long ago I cursed him an' wished him dead?

If Maya dies, how could I not avenge her death?

"Miz Rose, Mistah Ben, you be like a mother an' father to me, and you will always have a place with us. I know Maya would want you to be here, but why have you brought Jonathan?"

Although Rafe's question wasn't unforeseen, Ben answered uncomfortably and somewhat apologetically.

"Rose and I also feel that you and Maya are a son and daughter to us, and we did not intend to disturb you. Our Jonathan rescued the young woman with him from enslavement at Mosquito Inlet. They tell of the awful starvation and cruelty which the people there endure, and of a terrible illness that has taken the lives of many. They flee in fear of Mister Hatcher and the heartless overseers who now hunt them. We had to get them out of Saint Augustine quickly to elude Mister Hatcher, and as we traveled here, Rose and I were reminded of the time we hid Maya and brought her here. Last night we stayed with a friend of Sam's at a farm in Picolata, and the man gave Jonathan maps and a letter to help them get to the North, but if Jonathan can buy a horse at the village, another horse would help them greatly on their journey. I know Jonathan regrets his association with Mister Hatcher, and he has learned much since then. We didn't know that Maya's health had declined. I'm sorry Rafe. Would you have us leave?"

Humbled by Ben's explanation and the memories of similar experiences, Rafe exchanged his resentment for tolerance.

"No, your son seems a different man than the man I met some weeks ago. You have helped us many times, an' I thank you for the money from the sale of our crops. I will help you find a hoss."

"Thank you for your generous spirit, but stay close with Maya. Sam and Eyota can help Jonathan buy a horse, then he and Darian will be on their way as soon as is possible."

"I'm glad you're here, Mistah Ben, I have nevah been so worried nor so scared."

43.

The day began with a drizzling rain, and the change of the weather accentuated the change in the lives of the small group of mourners as the dreary grayness that permeated the air also filled their heavy hearts with the bleak gloom of loss.

Wrapped in the quilt that she and Rose had sewn, and placed lovingly in the plain wooden coffin that Rafe had made for her, Maya was carried to a mound in the woods a short distance from Rafe's cabin.

Long stems of white flowers picked by Eyota and Darian crowned the grave where Maya was laid to rest, and during a simple, but lovely and deeply emotional ceremony, Ruth sang a beautiful, heartfelt lullaby that her mother had sung to her.

As Ruth took the cloth that Maya had worn when she carried Eli, and tucked it in gently between the bouquets, tears ran unashamedly down Rafe's cheeks.

Stunned by grief, he stood at the foot of Maya's grave, with Ben and Noah at his side, ready to assist him if necessary.

Her eyes puffy from crying and lack of sleep, Rose looked tired while she held Eli, and beside her, Jonathan felt the pain of guilt for his part in causing the child to now be motherless.

The lonesome figure of Rafe affected Sam, and while he and Eyota shared their sadness in silence, Sam worried that being older, he might someday be the one to leave Eyota on her own.

While the circle of friends walked back to the cabin, Ruth and Noah sang a joyful song of faith and freedom, which was the tradition of their families, and the resonance of Noah's baritone voice gave a profound power to the song.

At the cabin, an array of dishes from Native made pemmican to fresh roasted fish covered the tabletop, but in a confusion of heartbreak and anger, Rafe had no interest in food.

When the light rain stopped, he lifted Eli up into his arms and took him out to the garden.

Ben followed shortly after, then waited for Rafe to

speak. It didn't take long. Rafe wanted to talk.

"Maya an' I shared only a slivah of time in this world, but that slivah of time was my life. I loved her when she was too young to say my name, an' I longed for her everah day we were forced to be apart. The memories of her love helped me to go on when I thought I couldn't survive another hour, an' there was a time when her courage saved my life. I believe she saved all of our lives that day."

"She did, Rafe. None of us will ever forget Maya's bravery and selflessness, and we shall be forever grateful. When someone is willing to give their life for yours, they be an extraordinary person."

"A man couldn't hope for a better or more beautiful wife. Her smile could turn my labor into pleasure, an' her love gave me a son. I'm thankful for our time together, but where is the fairness in her death? Why should an evil man like Hatcher live a long life when someone as wonderful as Maya is dealt barely more than a moment?"

Ben empathized like a father.

"For hundreds of years people have asked those questions when they lost someone young and dear. I have asked the same in the past, but I don't believe anyone will ever learn the answers."

Rafe tried to hold in the tears that brimmed his eyes.

"Maya an' I went through so much, we worked so hard an' loved all we could. It can't be fair. It can't be right."

"No, 'tisn't fair nor right. There are many things in life that are not fair. We can only choose to do right over wrong, then live on without regret for knowing we did the best we could, even when 'twas difficult to do, and no matter that others might not have done the same."

"But what is right? Is it right for Hatcher to live when Maya will nevah walk on this Earth again? Nevah hold her child to her breast nor lie with me again? Oh God! How long before I forget the sound of her voice, the smell of her neck, the feel of her skin? How could it be wrong to seek an eye for an eye? I want Hatcher's blood."

"Do not soil your hands with his foul blood. He is a violent and callous man, yet he did not intend to shoot Maya. He doesn't know that he did, but Rafe, you know the bullet found Maya by chance. You were wronged and tormented by Mister Hatcher, but do not allow your grief for Maya to turn you into the cruel brute that Mister Hatcher has made of himself. Give your anger time to pass, and your heart time to heal. Maya loved the kindness of your soul and the forgiveness in your nature. For Maya and your child, and for yourself, be the good man that I know you to be. You deserve a better fate than the one that lies ahead for Mister Hatcher. Trust that he will reap what he has sown.

44.

Dugal wasn't surprised when Constable Grimes came to his door, but neither was he pleased. He may have been a thief, but he wasn't entirely a fool, and he told the version of the story that Hatcher had hoped he would.

When Grimes returned to the jail, he ordered Hatcher to get his horse from Dugal and leave the city, but at Dugal's place, Hatcher mounted his horse and headed for the Stewart's.

Again, the house and barn were quiet except for the chickens, and Hatcher left the city to ride for Picolata.

Without the encumbrance of a wagon, Hatcher's ride took him only four hours, but he arrived at Fort Picolata near sunset, thirsty, exhausted and in pain.

When one of the soldiers at the fort sold him a bottle of ale, Hatcher drank it with the last of his dried meat, but the soldier assured him that the Stewarts hadn't been there, and Hatcher spent the night lying on his stomach on the ground outside of the fort.

- - - - -

In the morning, the commotion of the soldiers roused Hatcher awake, but the painful welts on his back made him resentful of the disturbance.

What do I do now? I can't go back to Saint Augustine, an' I won't go back to Mosquito Inlet till I have Jonathan and his wench in my rope.

Blasted runaways! Where the bloody hell are they?

If I were a runaway, I believe I'd take the road that winds north from here. The road that Jonathan an' I took south, and the road where a fine doe waits to be my dinner.

About an hour up the trail, Hatcher rode into the woods, then stood in one spot long enough to shoot a deer as it wandered by him.

He'd gutted the animal and was about to light a fire with his flint, when he heard a rustling in the brush and the sharp snap of a branch.

He started to move quietly over to his horse to get his rifle, but a loud, snarling growl in the scrub between him and his steed frightened them both.

Hatcher ran east toward the trail, but his horse fled in a northwest direction.

While Hatcher looked for his horse, he walked a wide circle to the river's edge, but his horse wasn't at the water as he'd supposed, and his calls and whistles seemed to fade into a hollow forest.

As he trudged northward, his search went fruitless, but with only a few hours of sunlight left to the day, need and hunger urged him on.

In anger, he muttered to the woods.

"I've been jailed an' whipped an' starved. My horse has run off with my rifle an' whip, an' most everythin' I own. I have no rope or blanket, and I walk through the wilderness with nothin' leave a knife, but the nastiest bit be that I have no rum or beer. Bloody hell, I'd rather lie in hell 'n drink stinkin' water. 'Tis Jonathan's fault, him an' his bloody servant whore. I'll see 'em rot for it!"

45.

An early morning mist brought the first cooler air of September and the first hint of the autumn to come.

Rose usually welcomed the change of seasons, but the noticeable passing of time deepened the sorrow she felt over Maya's death and the coming departure of Jonathan and Darian.

As sunrise lifted the haze from the woods and lit their camp outside of Rafe's cabin, Rose felt a bittersweet moment of love and loss while she helped Darian add a strip of material to Maya's spare skirt, to lengthen the hem.

Rafe had considered giving Maya's clothes to Ruth, but his tolerance for Jonathan had softened into a tentative friendship, and he'd decided that Darian needed the few pieces of clothing more.

While Rose and Darian sewed together, they were mostly silent, yet they grew closer in spirit, and Rose lamented,

"I wish you didn't have to leave. I shall miss you and my Jonathan, and I shall miss seeing the beautiful babies that you will bear."

In the excitement of sailing to a new world, Darian hadn't realized at the beginning how heartbroken she would be to never see her mother again, nor how sad she would feel to know that her mother would never see her daughter again nor ever see her grandchildren.

While Darian pined for her mother, Rose yearned for all of her daughters.

As the two women took on the roles of mother and daughter for each other, Darian tenderly assured Rose,

"When babies come, we will come to you."

Ben heard Darian's promise as he walked by with a bucket of well water, and he had to disagree.

"When babies come you must send a letter, and we shall come to you, but before you and Jonathan go north you must be able to ride a horse well. The trail you shall follow will be difficult. There shall be many water crossings without bridges, and unlike the flat land we have here, there shall be steep hills and deep valleys. Your horse may need to flee from danger, and you shall need to stay on your mount."

While Ben poured the water into a barrel, Jonathan walked into the camp with Sam and Eyota, and with the horse that they'd chosen for Darian at the village.

Bridled, and fitted with a man's saddle, which was hardly more than a slightly padded leather strap over a blanket, the small brown horse stood proud and beautiful; a near match for Jonathan's own.

Darian ran to Jonathan and hugged him, then she fondly petted the horse's velvety muzzle.

"This horse, I love. I ride."

Darian hadn't fully understood Ben's speech, and Jonathan misunderstood Darian.

Since she'd handled the ride well when they rode on his horse together, he believed she meant that she knew how to ride.

He boosted her up to sit astride, but when she wriggled in the saddle to adjust her skirt, she unintentionally gave the horse a kick, and it bolted.

After an awkward start, the horse took Darian down the path toward the road, and in seconds they were out of sight behind a bend of trees.

Even though there wasn't much of a saddle to hold onto, Darian managed to keep her feet in the stirrups and hang on, and she almost reached the trail before she yelled for help.

Until then, no one realized that Darian didn't know how to control a horse.

Jonathan's horse stood by the wagons with Amelia

and Henry, and although none of the horses were saddled, all were bridled.

With a giant leap, Jonathan mounted his horse's bare back and rode after Darian with all the speed that he could ask of his steed.

When his path met the trail, he saw Darian on her horse a good distance ahead to the south, but as he began to catch up to her, a horse without a rider come out of the woods and joined in the race behind Darian. A horse that Jonathan knew well.

Hatcher's horse! But where is Hatcher? Does he hide in the woods to attack us, or is he dead?

His horse pushes Darian's to run faster, but slows my own and brings a greater chance of harm to us.

I have only a mane to grip for balance. If I try to grab Darian and lift her from her horse, she might fall beneath the hooves of Hatcher's horse.

We both could fall and be trampled, but this trail is too narrow to force Darian's horse to turn. Her horse would likely run into a tree, and mine would run with it.

In three miles or so our horses will tire, but 'tis a long way, and I see how her ride batters her. She could be thrown at any moment.

I would take any risk for Darian, but what risk do I choose for her to take?

Hatcher, you loathsome scoundrel! Even your horse would murder us.

- - - - -

The welts on Hatcher's back pained him, and the whines of mosquitoes were as much a nuisance to him as the itch of their bites, but as the morning light cleared the mist, he continued to walk northward on the trail while he looked for his horse.

In an attempt to get food, he threw his knife at a bird, but when he missed, he almost lost the blade in the thick brush and he began to search more stridently for his horse.

When he heard the rumble of horses coming toward him from the north, he hoped to get food and help from their riders, and he waited for them by the side of the trail.

The horses were practically on top of him by the time he saw that his horse was one of them, and they were beside him when he recognized Jonathan, but they rode by Hatcher so closely and swiftly that his own horse nearly ploughed him over, and they were past him before he could think to act.

He yelled after them, but they kept going. He whistled hard and loud, and the ears of his horse twitched and turned, but his horse ran on with the others.

Bloody horse! He mocks me! A mongrel in a pack of dogs. I'll teach him what his disobedience will bring.

Intensely absorbed in passing Hatcher's horse and rescuing Darian, Jonathan caught only a glimpse of Hatcher just as the horses raced by him, but that brief glance told Jonathan that Hatcher was alive, and

Jonathan urged his horse to go faster.

- - - - -

Shortly after Jonathan rode off to rescue Darian, Rafe followed on Henry, but the unsaddled horse's large size and wide back made for an ungainly ride at a slower pace.

As Rafe rode down the trail, he remembered a time two years earlier when he'd ridden bareback to rescue Maya after she'd bravely gone with a bounty hunter, in order to save her friends lives and his own.

While Rafe relived the day, he came up behind a man running down the trail ahead of him and he slowed Henry's pace, but when he got close enough to see that the man was Hatcher, Rafe's heartache over Maya fueled his anger.

Rafe was about to leap from Henry's back onto Hatcher's when Hatcher also recognized Rafe, and he brandished his knife.

Although Rafe carried no weapons, he had the advantage of having a horse, and he chose to ride past Hatcher, but before Rafe could get by, Hatcher lunged out wildly with his blade.

In his attempt to cut Rafe and take him captive once again, Hatcher slashed Henry's flank instead.

Henry jumped and whinnied a guttural scream, and with a solid, crushing buck to Hatcher's chest, he knocked Hatcher forcefully to the ground.

Henry's kick also threw Rafe off of his back, but Rafe

landed in a patch of tall grass and soft sand beside the trail, where he needed only to catch his breath.

Hatcher had fallen on hard dirt a few feet away from his knife, but he'd already suffered the excruciating injuries of deep bruises and broken ribs from the horse's powerful buck, and he couldn't move.

Rafe picked up the knife and stood above Hatcher in a threatening stance, but when Hatcher tried to beg for his life, his words gurgled in his throat, and Ben's advice and prophecy repeated in Rafe's mind.

"I will not hurt you, Mistah Hatcher. I can't see the use in it. I'll get the doctah for you, but I don't believe you'll live to see him. To reap what you have sown is your fate."

- - - - -

Running at top speed, Jonathan's horse edged its way up to the front of the race. When he ran a nose ahead, Jonathan reached out to grab the bridle of Darian's horse, but the horses bumped and moved apart, and Jonathan's outstretched arm fell short of the prize.

Both he and Darian almost fell, but although the near fall frightened Darian, she held on.

Jonathan struggled to reclaim his seat, but as he regained control, he cautiously worked his steed further to the lead.

When he tried for the bridle again, he got hold of it, and as he pulled back on the bridle, he slowed his own horse to help reduce the speed of Darian's.

Hatcher's horse braked with them, and the three horses came to a stop together.

Their feet finally on the ground, Jonathan and Darian clung together in a long and ardent embrace. Eager for each other, and thankful for their lives, they kissed with all the fervor, passion and desire of young love.

As they walked the trail north to Rafe's cabin, the blue sky looked clearer and the fragrance of the forest seemed sweeter, and Jonathan kept an eye out for Hatcher.

"Our ordeal may not be over, Darian," Jonathan confessed, "we passed Hatcher a mile back on the road, but we have his horse and his rifle and whip, and I am ready for him."

- - - - -

Rafe walked Henry to his cabin to get care for him, and to tell everyone about his encounter with Mister Hatcher.

While Sam rode Amelia to the village to get the doctor for Hatcher, Ben and Rose tended to Henry, and Rafe headed back to the trail with Noah.

When the doctor rode up to the spot where Hatcher lay, Rafe and Noah had already arrived, but there was nothing that any of them could do for Hatcher. He had lain alone in the dirt in agony when his heart stopped beating.

Jonathan and Darian appeared down the trail as they made their way north with the horses, and while Rafe walked down to meet them, Jonathan saw the doctor and Noah standing about where he last saw Hatcher.

"Is there trouble? I saw Hatcher here when we rode past him. Has he hurt someone?"

"Yes," Rafe nodded, "he hurt Henry, by the slash of a blade meant for me, but Henry bested Mistah Hatcher with an almighty kick, an' Mistah Hatcher will never hurt anyone again."

46.

There was nothing special about Hatcher's burial. No marker, no flowers or friends, but as Jonathan and Rafe dug a hole in the woods together, they came to accept each other as brothers; sons of Ben and Rose.

They divided up Hatcher's belongings between them. The horse, saddle and blanket to Rafe, and the rifle, whip and knife to Jonathan.

They gave the rope and leather purse to Ben, the empty flask to Sam, and the clothes to Noah and Ruth, to be remade for the children. The boots were set aside for the village doctor, even though Rafe thought that they wouldn't fit him.

In the early evening, the two young men sat on Rafe's small porch, and while their family and friends sat around them, Sam reluctantly told news that he'd waited for the right time to tell.

"'Twas rumored in the village today that the elders believe a tribal war is coming, and they are going to move the village south, deeper into Florida."

A chorus of shocked gasps accompanied Rose's.

"A war? Dear Lord. The entire village? So many friends and family leaving at once? Oh no! Everything will change, and I have hoped that Jonathan and Darian would raise their family here. Here, where I could watch their children grow with Eli, and Noah and Ruth's child."

Sam looked at the group of stunned and unhappy faces.

"Tis merely hearsay," he said, but the damage had been done. There wasn't a person on the porch who didn't feel disturbed about the move or the possibility of war.

Slightly defiant, but mostly determined, Rafe stood up to declare himself.

"When the villagers go, I will go with them. I am young an' strong, an' they will need me to help them build. I will build a bigger cabin for Eli an' me, an' I will help to build a better village for the friends who helped me an' Maya."

Noah and Ruth shared a look, and without

hesitation, Noah agreed.

"We will go with you."

Jonathan had made up his mind before he'd heard Sam's news.

"I'm sorry Mother, but Darian and I must go north, to Charles Town or farther. If Hatcher could find us here so quickly, other hunters might find us wherever we may be in Florida. Regardless of whether we change our names or present the letter from Boyd Lawson, 'tis too dangerous for us to remain in Florida."

Rose knew that Jonathan spoke the truth, but while she felt heartsick over the prospect of her children and her friends leaving, Ben took it in stride.

"I shall miss you all. Especially you, Jonathan, and you, Rafe. If ever you are in need of anything, Rose and I shall always want to help you and our grandchildren. And Noah, I also say this to you and Ruth. Do you have enough money, Jonathan, to make this journey with Darian? At this time," he held up Hatcher's empty purse, "money is the one thing I am unable to offer."

Jonathan jingled the coins that he had left in his pouch and spilled them out onto a little table next to Darian, where she sat on the edge of the porch.

After giving several coins to Rose for purchases in St. Augustine, slipping a few to the guards at the city gate, and spending an amount to buy Darian a horse, Jonathan's cache had dwindled.

Darian looked at the scattered coins on display at her eye level, and when one with a familiar shape and cut to its edge stood out, her eyes opened wide.

My coin!

Amazed, she picked up the coin and held it tightly as she clasped it against her heart.

"My coin! I find in water in Saint Augustine. I wished on it, Jonathan, I wished for love."

The love between Darian and Jonathan shone like the golden glow of the evening's sunset, and everyone there felt the glorious tingle of the miracle of love.

The moment calmed Rose's fear of the changes to come, and soothed the rawness of Rafe's sad loss.

Sam put his arm around Eyota, and Noah gently rubbed Ruth's growing belly.

Love had prevailed, and love would get them through, no matter what the future might bring.

Jonathan helped Darian up from the porch, and as they stood closely together, he looked deeply into her eyes.

"The first time I saw you, you were standing at the landing in Saint Augustine, wringing seawater from your skirt. I fell in love with you then, and I knew I would always love you. Come north with me, Anna."

As she looked up into his eyes, everything and everyone but him, disappeared into the glow.

"My coin, my wish," she smiled tenderly, "I wished for you, Aedan."

J.S. Lavallee

If you have ever wanted to write, but you put it off because you were too busy, write now.

Don't wait for that moment when you have nothing to do. Life rarely seems to get quiet, there's always something.

Take those bits and pieces of your life that you've collected, shuffle them like cards, arrange them into an over-the-top crossword puzzle that sits inside of a wild jigsaw puzzle, and write.

Look yourself in the eye and tell yourself that you can do it.

Sure, it might not be easy, but you'll feel wonderful.

Start with the seed of something that happened to you along the way, and see where it leads you.

I found the inspiration to write my first book, *A Slice of Moon*, when a young runaway came to my door in St. Augustine one morning and asked for a ride.

I could tell she was younger than she claimed to be, and she was hungry and scared. My husband and I fed her, and helped her to get back to her family, but while I sat on the front porch talking with her, I felt as if I'd been taken back in time and the story came to me.

When I began to write the sequel, *A Sliver of Time*,

I thought of the time in Key West when I made a wish for love as I buried an old Spanish coin near the ocean.

The coin was a bit of two that had been given to me as a gift from the famous treasure hunter, Mel Fisher, back in the 1970's when I served drinks on the beach at the infamous Chart Room Bar.

Fifteen years later, on my third date with Joe (my husband now for almost 30 years), Joe began to tell me a story of how he'd found a coin near the ocean with his metal detector, under a full moon.

I told him to stop right there. I remembered the unusual shape of my coin and I made a sketch of it while I told him where he'd found it.

It was my coin. Joe had found it three months before we met, and I'd been trying to meet him for three months, since the day I first saw him, when he walked by my window with his golden retriever.

I've written a short, true story all about it, for my next book.

The world has been through a lot this year, and our troubles with the covid-19 virus and the pain it has caused so many, may be with us for some time to come. My photo shows me with my mask. I wear it because I would rather help someone than hurt anyone. I support and applaud the doctors, nurses and first responders who are true heroes of our time, and I thank anyone who has done anything to help.

Made in the USA
Columbia, SC
05 November 2020

23994354R00159